Cry Tough
A Novel

Love is all you need

Olevi
1/3/15

OLIVE ROSE STEELE

A REVIEW

In Blossom Mae Black, Olive Rose Steele has created an unforgettable heroine who evokes comparisons to one of literary fiction's most memorable characters—Scarlett O'Hara. Beautiful and brazen 'Bloss,' as she is called by those who love her in spite of her flaws and poor choices, is infuriating and endearing at the same time. If you are conservative, she will shock you. If you are a hopeless romantic, she will appeal to your heart. And if you are adventurous, prone to grab at life and ride every opportunity towards your shifting goals, well then, Bloss will get into your head and haunt you. You will want to step into her life story and make things okay. You are concerned for her. Fear for her. Want to be her and yet not want to be her. That is the strength of Steele's writing craft. Highly believable fiction. *Cry Tough* is a poignant story that will stay with you long after you have read through the entire novel, and reread the beginning—which is a *must* to bring closure to your own keening emotions—and have closed the book, and put it away.

- Cheryl Antao-Xavier, author
  Publisher, In Our Words Inc.

Cry Tough
A Novel

OLIVE ROSE STEELE

This book is a work of fiction. Some names of actual places have been included. Similarities to actual persons or events are entirely coincidental. All depictions are the product of the author's imagination.

Book cover designed by Shirley Aguinaldo
Book cover photo by Geoffery Gordon Goldswain, Dreamstime.com

Copyright © 2011 Olive Rose Steele

All rights reserved.

ISBN-13:978-0981072319
ISBN-10:0981072313
Published in 2014

Cry Tough: A Novel / Olive Rose Steele

For information contact: Blackwood
78-3035 Artesian Drive, Mississauga, Ontario L5M 7S7
e-mail: letshave_coffee@ymail.com

First Edition: August, 2014
Printed in the USA

for Sharon

CONTENTS

PROLOGUE I	1
PROLOGUE II	5
PART ONE (1977-1987)	8
PART TWO (1987-2002)	160
PART THREE (2002-2009)	225
EPILOGUE (2011)	270

PROLOGUE I
Ethica Mature Lifestyles, 2010

Blossom Mae Black had become a shadow of her former self. Those who knew this beautiful, vibrant, fun-loving woman thought she was dead. But she was alive and quietly living in an exclusive locale on the banks of Lake Ontario, just outside of Toronto. Blossom loved to be in the beautiful rose garden at *Ethica Mature Lifestyles.* Sitting next to a cluster of red rose bushes, she contemplated her life—loves lost and gained, missed opportunities, and magnificent successes. Her eyes caught the framed photograph of her late son, Jason, at age three months, set upright on a small table beside her. Today, Jason would have been twenty-four years old, about six feet tall, with broad shoulders, just like his father. He might have been the ideal husband to a maiden of Blossom's imagination. She swallowed to clear inflammation that had formed in her throat—a side effect from daily medicine. Blossom's mind flitted through decades of thoughts, some of which brought her joy and others that she scorned. Some scenes were static, others played like a broken record. And it seemed like yesterday that her world, at least in her mind, had been turned upside down. Blossom tugged on the warm afghan in her lap—she remembered....

The phone rang. Lorna Jones grabbed it quickly. "Hello? For you, Blossom."

"Hello, this is Blossom."

"Hi, Bloss. How are you?"

Her heart skipped several beats when she recognized the voice to be that of Sheldon Morgan. They had not spoken for a year, yet she felt as if she were continuing a conversation she'd started with Sheldon the evening before. She imagined him—lean and muscular. He didn't have to work out, for his occupation provided the exercise he needed to maintain his physique. He was likely standing, holding the phone in a casual way. She pictured his dimpled chin close to the mouthpiece and his strong fingers curved around the handle. She remembered his scent, his gentle touch. She wondered if his wife Maureen was with him. Where was he calling her from? Why hadn't he called before? Did he not know she'd been waiting for this moment?

"I am well, Sheldon," Blossom said.

Lorna Jones turned around sharply. "You want me to handle this call?" Lorna mimed.

"No," Blossom mimed back.

"Maureen and I are in Toronto, on our way to Niagara Falls, for a holiday. I couldn't go back to Montego Bay without seeing you ... I don't know, perhaps have lunch this afternoon?" Sheldon said.

Fresh tears began to roll down Blossom's cheeks, curving under her chin and landing between her breasts. Her heart was beating out of control. She was not sure whether she should be angry at Sheldon or just be indifferent. Her knees buckled, her hands shook and her eyes went dark with tears. She leaned back against the kitchen cupboard with the phone pressed to her ear, her lips moved but the words were silent.

I'll be doggone if I didn't tell you how I've been, Sheldon Morgan ... I've been sick with grief over the death of my child, your son ... the son I conceived with you and delivered in secret. Perhaps there's a price I must pay for such an ill-conceived plan ... for fate has chased me down, got into my face and made me regret. This is the price I paid for loving you.

Blossom's tears kept rolling down her cheeks.

Her silence was disquieting.

"Did I call you at a bad time?"

"It is truly a bad time Sheldon, I am preparing to attend a funeral this afternoon," Blossom answered, hoping to dismiss him quickly.

"A funeral?"

"Yes ... it's unfortunate that I give you bad news, I cannot keep this fact a secret any longer, our son ... the son I conceived with you will be buried today."

"*Our* son," Sheldon repeated, after a long pause. He was evidently knocked for six. He released a sigh, then he stuttered, "May I see you this afternoon, Bloss?"

The phone fell from Blossom's hand. Lorna Jones picked it up. "Hello? ... Mr. Morgan? I'm sorry sir, Miss Black has said goodbye." Lorna returned the phone to its cradle.

"Come, Blossom ... pull yourself together ... be strong." Lorna consoled her as she brushed tears from Blossom's cheeks with the back of her hands.

Giving birth to the child of Sheldon Morgan was exactly what Blossom Black had planned. It was true, the consequences of her plan to bear Sheldon's child would ruin lives and cause untold heartaches, but Blossom had been resolute, she would only be content with an outward sign of her love for him. Had it been worth the price?

PROLOGUE II
Montego Bay, 1977

She made a wish and then swung a pebble out to sea. The pebble skimmed over the surface of the water before it sank; she smiled at her trick as she walked along the beach to her perfect hideaway.

In Montego Bay, the seasons are the same—sunny days, warm afternoons, and cool nights, except those hazy, rainy days that made her wish for a new life, in a country where spring, summer, fall and winter looked and felt different. The sun was majestic. There was not a cloud in the blue sky. She stood at the pinnacle of a rock that had been molded into the earth by nature, overlooking white sands.

Apart from her own private waterfall, this rock was where she spent many hours, wishing and hoping. The ocean breeze was cool, the mist salty. She inhaled several deep breaths as she surveyed the landscape. Sangster International Airport was plainly visible through the glistening sunlight; planes landed and took off. Vehicles that looked like toys moved in and out of the airport parking lot. People meandered on the beach and the white sands massaged their feet. She turned her head slowly toward the endless expanse of water in front of her. Far out was the silver skyline—she saw a shiny speck at the edge of the ocean, probably a cruise ship or a banana boat sailing by too quickly to tell if it was moving.

Blossom Mae Black was twenty-seven years old, average height, slender, green eyes and long black hair. She had big dreams and great aspirations and imagined living in a foreign country—England or the United States, maybe even Canada. She pictured a life of success, opulence, and fame on a level that her father, a popular musician, and her mother, a ballet dancer, had never achieved. She had a business degree, but her world saw her as a glorified administrative assistant and Blossom intended to change that view.

"Life is good here. You will be happier when you find a job," Whitfield Norman Black told his daughter. "And the boy you've been dating, Gerald Morgan's son, he seems like a fine young man. I see good qualities in him. It's time you settle down. Give me grandchildren," her father said.

"Daddy, your thoughts are running away with you," Blossom had responded.

Blossom was steadfast; she believed someday, soon, a brighter future would unfold. For now, she would wait for the right break at the right time.

PART ONE

1977 – 1987

*For even as love crowns you so shall he crucify you. Even as he is for your growth so is he for your pruning.
Even as he ascends to your height and caresses your tenderest branches that quiver in the sun, so shall he descend on your roots and shake them in their clinging to the earth.*

—*Kahlil Gibran*, The Prophet.

ONE
Yorkville, Toronto

Fall of 1977 had been unseasonably warm—a real Indian summer. Hansel Smith and Clinton Gayle sat at a small table, on the sidewalk patio at Muff's Café sipping cool drinks and talking. Hansel's glass of tonic water toppled over. "Damn, this happens every time. Those pretty women walking by make me nervous." He turned and looked at Clinton with glazed-over eyes. "So, when will the girl from Montego Bay arrive?"

"You mean Blossom Black?"

"Yes, Blossom Black, when will she get here?"

Clinton studied Hansel. "Hans, don't be getting big ideas, the deal we made is strictly business. You do your part and the rest will fall into place, Blossom has her own plans, she isn't looking for a relationship."

"No worries, Clint, everything is cool, I'm only interested in my share of the dough … got to pay bills, my friend."

Hansel had always imagined himself a performer. His mother saw him as the son, who could be—a doctor, a lawyer, a teacher, even a businessman, nevertheless he was a blues singer.

Hansel had never been interested in formal schooling even though his father had told him, "Finish your education. Don't end up being a street entertainer like me … earning a pittance."

Everyone who was familiar the Smith family from Pond Street in Sheffield, England, knew that the father played a guitar, the mother played cymbals, and Hansel—the little boy—sang along with the mother; no one was surprised that Hansel sang blues when he became a man.

"I love to sing blues. Singing anything but blues is a waste of my talent," Hansel told his friends. He was at his best when he was performing his B.B. King imitations.

When Hansel took up residence in Toronto, he was a grown man and an established blues singer, but work was hard to come by except for the occasional gigs at the El Mocambo nightclub. Hansel was a notorious flirt, and his British accent attracted the ladies. He would often say he loved women, fine "things," and his music—in that order.

What Hansel lacked in brainpower he made up for in smoothness—which was why he jumped at the opportunity when he read an ad at a local grocery store for a male live-in companion.

"And I don't have to pay room and board? I like that," Hansel had said with a wide grin when his friend Clinton cautioned him about the ad.

Hansel had gotten the job and stayed in the employ of divorcee Mavis Brennan who was bent on keeping up her extra-curricular activities with a handsome man on her arm. And even though Mavis was pleased with her hire, she was taken aback when Hansel demanded additional compensation if she required him to escort her on social events. Moreover, requests for sexual favors were met with expectations of an expensive gift.

Muff's Café was bustling. Clinton looked closely at Hansel; he noticed blues in his eyes and he wondered if his friend was truly a happy man.

"Hans, you don't visit me and Darlene often enough ... Don't be a stranger."

"Mavis keeps me busy, my friend ... Cheerio Buddy." Hansel said and disappeared into Yorkville's late afternoon crowd.

TWO

When Darlene Gayle and her husband Clinton settled in Toronto five years earlier, Darlene had intended to complete her nursing education at McMaster University. But she'd shelved her dream of becoming a nurse and obtained temporary work as a clerk at a freight forwarding company in Toronto. They had invested the savings they brought with them from Sheffield in the purchase of a modest three-bedroom bungalow on Jane Street.

"Money's been tight since the tenants moved out last year," Darlene said. She'd been moaning over lack of sufficient funds to keep up the family.

"We'll fix the leak in the basement and renovate the place to make it suitable for renting," Clinton had reassured Darlene. "And when your cousin Blossom comes, we'll charge her room and board for the guest room." he went on.

Darlene and Blossom had been pen-pals. They'd exchanged letters and photos at every stage of their childhood and the habit continued even as they became adults. Darlene had sent Blossom several snapshots of Toronto skyscrapers; shots of her home; and larger shots of herself sitting at her snazzy desk, at work. Darlene's Toronto life in photographs fascinated Blossom.

"Darlene, I've decided, Toronto is where I want to live." Blossom had relayed in a letter to Darlene.

"The winters are cold. You'll miss the year-round summers you enjoy in Montego Bay." Darlene had tried to deter Blossom but she would not be put off.

"I'm not troubled by the change in temperature Darlene, I'm ready to experience a different kind of weather ... I shall see you soon," Blossom had communicated in a letter.

"Promise me you'll be wearing a cardigan and a pair of warm shoes when I pick you up at the airport," Darlene had written back.

"I promise," Blossom had replied.

Darlene had chuckled, knowing that in all likelihood, Blossom would experience melancholy over her first few winters away from home even if she kept it a secret.

"Some people get stressed out from the change," Darlene had said to Clinton in a discussion about how well Blossom might acclimatize to a foreign country.

* * *

Blossom Black walked out to passenger pick-up at Pearson Airport on October 12, 1977 to be received by her cousin Darlene. The wind that whirled around her long floral dress on that bright fall day seemed not as chilly as Darlene had cautioned, granted she was wearing a cardigan over her shoulders. And her wedge heel flip-flops turned out to be adequate protection for her feet. She was about to hail a cab when someone called out, "Blossom!" When she turned around she recognized Darlene.

"My car is in the parking garage across the street; let's load up your stuff." Darlene carried Blossom's duffle bag and hefted it into the trunk of her car. She clicked the trunk shut. Blossom climbed into the front passenger seat next to her. They exited the airport. In a short time, they were driving around in busy Toronto.

Blossom peered out the window from time to time to see what was happening on the streets. A bus careened on rails in the middle of the road. Farther along, traffic veered off to the side to give way to an oncoming fire truck. A police car and an ambulance followed closely behind the fire truck. The scene was chaotic. It did not matter. It was the beginning of her new life. Blossom inhaled the air that blew in through the half-open window and caught a mixture of rich smells coming from an outdoor fruit market. *I will make this place my home*, she said to herself.

After several turns, unscheduled traffic stops, and pauses at bright red traffic lights, Darlene said, "Blossom, we're home." Blossom recognized a colorful garland at the top of the front door of Darlene's Jane Street bungalow. Clinton appeared. He put Blossom's luggage in the house.

Later, when Blossom was relaxing with a cup of hot chocolate, Darlene asked her, "How was your flight into Toronto?"

"It was bumpy for a while after we left Montego Bay," she answered.

Clinton entered the room as Blossom was finishing her account of the bumpy ride out of Montego Bay. "How was your flight, Blossom?" Clinton asked. She repeated the bumpy-ride story for Clinton.

"Welcome to our home. You got here safely, and that's all that matters to us." Clinton was smiling broadly.

Forty kilometers west of Darlene's bungalow, Hansel Smith sat in front of his television watching the sports channel and contemplating a business deal he'd agreed to with Clinton. The plan could fetch him one thousand fast dollars. He swung one leg over the side of his easy chair, drew in a mouth full of smoke from his cigarette and puffed out. The ring from his phone jolted him.

"Hello?"

"Hello Hans, Clinton here, don't forget, you're invited to our home on Sunday at four o'clock."

Clinton handed the phone to Darlene. "Hansel, you get your butt over here on Sunday and be on time," she snapped. "I certainly will, Darlene."

The Sunday after Thanksgiving was balmy. Around four o'clock, friends of Darlene and Clinton started to arrive for Blossom's welcome reception. Blossom was introduced to Kevin and Shirley Campbell; Justin Beckford and his fiancée Sophia Mais; Valarie Harper and Trevor Harrison; Alice and Austin Shields, and their two-year-old daughter Lee-Ann; and Hansel Smith and Mavis Brennan.

Sophia and Justin talked at length about their upcoming wedding. "We plan to spend our honeymoon in the Dominican Republic. My Dad collected thousands of air miles ... he offered them to Justin and me and we plan to use them to pay for our air fare." Sophia said.

"How nice," said Valarie. " ... I am sure Trevor and I will benefit from *his* air miles ...Trevor travels a lot on company business."

Hansel turned to Trevor, "You're still working for IBM, Trev?"

"Yes, I've been with IBM ten years now." Trevor answered.

Mavis and Alice were with Darlene in the dining room fussing over the seating arrangement around the dining table. *I'll put Blossom to sit across from Hansel,*

Darlene mused as she set a large dish with fresh fruits on the side table. "There, everything's copacetic!" She said aloud.

Austin was holding baby Lee-Ann as he conversed with Clinton about his recent purchase of a three-bedroom bungalow on Lakeshore Road.

"I plan to fix-up the basement and make it suitable for rental," Austin said.

"Good thinking man." Clinton said.

"Dinner is served," Darlene announced.

All of them sat down to eat.

"Scrumptious," Blossom whispered to Darlene.

"Catered," Darlene whispered back.

Sitting directly across from Hansel, Blossom noticed his dreadlocks were tied in a ponytail at the nape of his neck. He touched his chin frequently with his left hand, likely to show off the Rolex watch on his wrist. Earlier, when Hansel and Mavis had arrived, Darlene had whispered to Blossom, "They live together, you know."

"Who?"

"Those two," Darlene had said, tilting her head in the direction of Mavis and Hansel.

"They're an item?"

"Platonic."

"Good for her."

"How was your flight into Toronto Blossom?" Hansel asked her when the dinner chatter had died down. Blossom considered re-telling the same bumpy-ride-out-of-Montego Bay story. Instead she gave a different but equally true account of her experience. "The flight was smooth coming out of Montego Bay, except for a few bumps here and there. We arrived at Pearson on time and everyone applauded when we landed."

After dinner, all of them relaxed in Darlene's living room and listened to Hansel singing renditions of his favorite blues singer, B.B. King.

When the invited guests had left, Blossom sat by the fireside and contemplated her long-term plans. She was willing to pursue any option that would allow her to stay in Toronto on a permanent basis, and one such option was to marry someone who already had permanent status and then divorce him as soon as her permanent papers were finalized; an idea her boyfriend in Montego Bay pointedly pushed back.

Darlene was ready to proceed with the business of making sure Blossom stayed in Toronto. She clapped her hands. Clinton, Mavis, Hansel and Blossom looked in her direction. She pointed to a large pot of tea and several cups on a side table.

"Let's have tea and discuss the plan."

Hansel's eyes were bright with excitement.

"I've already agreed to my part of the deal," Hansel said.

Blossom was nervous. She shifted to the edge of her seat. Her recurring dream in which she was arriving at a passenger train station after the train had pulled out was playing almost nightly in her sleep. She feared her dream was foretelling a disappointment.

Clinton looked at Darlene. "I know a pastor who will do the marriage bit, his name is Bertram Lawrence. It's a quick and easy way for Blossom to stay permanently." He went on, "All Blossom has to do is marry Hansel, and then wait for the papers to arrive."

"Clinton, I told you before, Bloss does not like the *marriage* part," Darlene countered.

"It won't work any other way, Darlene. The marriage is just one piece of the whole *thing* and it takes about six months to completion. It is simple; Blossom or Hansel can initiate a divorce any time after they've received the official papers."

"It will cost money though," Hansel said.

"Why will it cost money?" Blossom inquired.

Hansel pursed his lips and looked at Clinton with narrowed eyes.

"It will cost *you* money because it's a business deal," Clinton quickly answered Blossom.

Darlene looked at Mavis and said. "Mavis, you make sure Hansel is okay with the plan."

"Hansel likes to have extra money in his pocket, he'll stick with it," Mavis assured Darlene.

"How much will it cost?" Blossom persisted.

"We'll get back to you on that later," Clinton answered quickly.

"Let's have more tea," Darlene said and refilled everyone's cup. She was obviously pleased with the discussions so far.

Blossom considered the players involved in the

plan; Clinton had not worked since his last temp assignment sorting mail at the post office and Darlene's income was not enough to maintain their lifestyle. Hansel's cut might be good for him since he hadn't had a singing gig for a long time. And, if everything goes according to the plan, she would be on a path to realizing her dream.

Two weeks later, on a cool Saturday afternoon, Darlene, Clinton, Hansel, and Blossom arrived in Clinton's Thunderbird car, at Pastor Lawrence's bungalow on Bathurst Street.

"Damn, we would've been here an hour ago if it hadn't been for those out-of-order traffic lights along the way and the detour on Spadina Street," Clinton said as he carefully parked his car at a curbside parking meter and slid some coins in the slot.

They walked into the living room of the pastor's house, set up like the inside of a church. A podium was fixed on a raised platform, a large portrait of Jesus hung on the wall behind the podium, and a vase filled with artificial flowers mounted on a nearby pedestal.

A side door opened sharply.

Fragrance drifted into the room.

Pastor Bertram Lawrence strode in like there was an entourage behind him.

"Hello, people," he said.

Blossom jumped back. "He scared me."

"Relax … He didn't mean to startle you. It'll be okay," Darlene assured her.

Pastor Lawrence had been holding church services in the living room of his residence on Bathurst Street since he broke away from the main church body with some of the congregation. He was wearing his customary light blue seersucker summer suit and white shirt. His dark blue necktie matched the handkerchief tucked in his jacket pocket. He beckoned the group to the podium. Darlene reached into her handbag, pulled out an envelope and handed it to Pastor Lawrence; he slid the envelope into a wooden box by the side of his podium.

"Who has the ring?" Pastor Lawrence asked.

"There's no ring," Darlene answered and signaled the Pastor to proceed.

"Let's get started," Pastor Lawrence said, pulling out a sheet of typewritten paper from the belly of his podium. He looked over his eyeglasses at Blossom, "Say after me ..."

Blossom repeated the last obligatory "I do" and breathed a sigh of relief. She was glad the act was over. She was ready to run for the door when she noticed Darlene frantically rummaging through her handbag.

"I forgot to bring the camera," Darlene said.

"No photos," Hansel said.

"We need to have photos ... photos are part of the documentation," Darlene said.

It did not matter to Blossom that Darlene had put the certificate from the Pastor in her handbag; she was relieved to be done with this part of the plan.

Darlene looked at Blossom with a smile, "I'll keep the certificate, Clinton and I will handle the immigration stuff."

They skipped out of the Pastor's living room/church and hurried to Clinton's car. There was a parking ticket on his windshield.

"Those spiteful cops are at it again ... All they do is hang around and wait for the meter to expire and then they slap a parking fine on a man's car." Clinton was furious.

Several weeks passed before news circulated that individuals, including Pastor Lawrence had been named in a law suit involving false immigration documents.

"I would've been naïve if I'd believed you were not involved in the scam," Blossom said to Darlene.

"It might sound unbelievable but I too was shocked when I found out that Clinton and Hansel were part of the trick. I would certainly not have agreed to such a plan had I known the truth," Darlene confessed.

Blossom was disappointed that her cousin on whom she had pinned her hopes to succeed had duped her. She considered her father's option of returning home to a settled life with her boyfriend in Montego Bay. But that was not to be; because, around the same time, news broke about a general official pardon for undocumented migrants. The pardon had given Blossom the break she needed to go forward.

Blossom considered it might be time to find a job so she picked up a newspaper at a corner box and looked over the want ads. Her eyes dropped down to a small ad at the bottom of the classified page that read: *Toronto Law firm seeks competent personnel assistant.* She was competent, so she pursued the opportunity. Not long after that she was interview and placed on a waiting list to be considered for the job.

If Blossom had had misgivings that her future plans had gone off the rails she was, at that moment, certain everything had been back on track.

THREE

Ronald Austin Johnson, thirty-years old, shrewd, intelligent, and appealing. He was successor to his father's patent and trademark law firm, Johnson, Johnson & Lindsay. He'd already been married and divorced once although he vowed he would be *married to the law* forever. He carried with him an arrogance that said, "Hello world: I'm here! Take me!"

Ron's mother's French–Canadian heritage and his father's mix of Italian and British lineage accounted for his tall, dark, and handsome features. The tautness of his form showed he took care of himself, although he walked with a slight limp from a bad car accident that happened when he was an out-of-control teenager who was driving too fast.

"There isn't a lot of money to be made in patent and trademark cases," Ron had said to his father upon his graduation from law school. He was determined to transform the firm to a combination of corporate, criminal, and family law practice, "and patent and trademark to keep my father happy," he'd said to his mother. And, given his tough, brazen, in-your-face style, it was no surprise that he wanted to be a successful criminal defense lawyer.

When Seymour Johnson entered Ron's office and sat on the edge of the huge cherry wood desk he'd given him when he completed law school a year earlier, Ron could tell right away that his father was about to be his usual matter-of-fact self.

"Son … As you know, I've been searching for a personnel assistant to replace Elaine Moore," Seymour said, handing Ron the folder he was holding. "I interviewed Miss Blossom Black," Seymour continued, rubbing his chin as though rethinking the decision. "Miss Black represented herself very well at the interview, and from talking with her references, I've established that she's qualified to do the job." Despite his good sense, Seymour Johnson seemed to be somewhat hesitant about his decision to hire Blossom Black.

"Get to the point, Dad," Ron said impatiently.

"Give her a call and offer her the job."

Ron slowly leafed through several pages in the folder. "Dad," he exclaimed, "she is an Island girl; she probably has no Canadian work experience and an accent that will drive you crazy."

His father frowned, several furrows appearing on his forehead.

"Good heavens, Ron, how will this Island girl who probably has an accent that will drive me crazy get Canadian work experience if someone doesn't hire her?"

Confident that he could depend on his son to make a proper assessment of the matter, Seymour's frown turned into a smile.

"Very well, Dad, I'll give her a call."

"Thank you, son." Seymour retreated from his son's office and closed the door quietly behind him.

Blossom sat next to the telephone on the wall in her cousin's kitchen waiting to hear if she'd got the job at Johnson, Johnson & Lindsay. Seymour Johnson, the CEO, had told her he'd be interviewing more applicants and he'd have an answer for her soon.

One afternoon, a week after the interview, the phone rang. "May I speak with Miss Black?" The male caller said.

"This's she," Blossom said.

"My name is Ron … I'm calling from Johnson, Johnson & Lindsay to tell you Mr. Seymour Johnson has offered you the position of personnel assistant. If you are available, he would like you to report for work Monday morning." There was a note of finality in Ron Johnson's voice.

"Thank you, sir ... I will be at work on Monday." Blossom was thrilled. The job could not have come at a better time. She dialed her father long distance.

"Daddy, I got the job!"

"I'm proud of you baby, when do you start?"

"I start on Monday, Daddy!"

Ron Johnson had to be in his office that Monday morning by nine o'clock. He entered the lobby of his office building with a gust of wind following him and, in no mood to greet anyone, headed straight to the elevators. The elevators were slow. Impatient, he pushed the up button several times in hopes that the doors would instantly fly open. Nothing happened. A movement in the corner of one eye caught Ron's attention, and he turned around to see a new face: She had light-brown skin; perfectly arched eyebrows that highlighted her bright green eyes; long black hair that flowed down her back; and a well-proportioned body that would attract the saintliest of men.

Who is this woman? The thought lingered in Ron's mind. He had been a tenant in the building long enough to recognize a new face. Ron was not one to hold back; when he wanted an answer, he asked a question. Was she on business? Was she visiting someone? *No need to speculate; just approach and inquire,* he thought. He walked directly to where Blossom had been standing.

"The elevators are slow this morning," he said in her hearing distance. She did not respond.

Ron was annoyed by the woman's silence. Not used to being ignored, he moved away. An elevator going up opened, and people hurried in and pressing the buttons on the elevator panel. The new woman searched the panel for the right button.

"What floor?" Ron asked her.

"Fourteen," she answered.

She talks, and she has an accent ... She must be Blossom Black, he said to himself.

Ron and Blossom exited the elevators on the fourteenth floor. He pulled open the huge double glass door entrance into his suite of offices, "After you, ma'am."

FOUR

It was eight o'clock in the morning. David Olson Clark peered through the glass panel in the front door of his North York bungalow, looking for a hint that the fog had let up—the fog was thick. Traffic along Don Valley Parkway would be a nightmare.

"Here's your coffee, honey," his wife Clara handed him a cup and saucer three quarters full of coffee to avoid an accidental spill.

Dressed in dark gray business suit and tie, and starched white shirt, David examined himself in the hall mirror—a slight paunch was showing, but a *man on a galloping horse* would not notice. David's personal trainer, Sonny, was working hard to flatten his stomach. *Too much beer,* he said to himself as he tightened his belt around his waist.

David had been mulling over the idea of

developing the land he'd bought in Etobicoke three years earlier. He examined the document he held in his hand and decided it was time to move forward with plans for expansion, although Clara had insisted the idea needed to mature some more.

"Camille," he called out from the living room, "bring me the keys to the Jeep."

"Camille drove the Jeep this morning, honey," Clara reminded him.

Ah, yes, he remembered; he'd allowed his daughter Camille to drive the Jeep to the family cottage in Collingwood.

He snapped his attaché case shut. He was scheduled to meet with his banker in thirty minutes.

"Good luck at the bank, hon," Clara said. She blew David a kiss as he stepped out into the chilly morning.

Two decades earlier, David had begun an occupation as a bricklayer, working on residential construction sites. He had taken on small- and medium-sized contracts, designing basements, building decks and patios, and performing general home repairs. His enterprising ways had led him to purchase and renovate homes and cottages, and re-sell them for profit. And the housing boom in Ontario had increased his business to the point of hiring tradespeople.

David's good luck had persisted with the discovery of lands in Jamaica, willed to him by his late father, that contained mineral sands and stones which he had been mining and manufacturing into granite and marble.

As David predicted, traffic was bumper to bumper along Don Valley Parkway. Fog lights and the weak morning sun competed to provide visibility. David breathed a sigh of relief when he arrived at his appointment without a fender bender.

"Good morning Tina, how was the commute into work this morning?" David asked bank manager Tina Jarrett, confident that a polite greeting would warm the chill he felt as he sat across from her. She observed him over her horn-rimmed glasses, her gaze locked onto his, searching for a reason not to accommodate any request he was about to make.

"I always walk to work, Mr. Clark ... I live five minutes from here." She put on a half-smile.

David Clark was not generally a nervous man, but Tina Jarrett gave him butterflies in his stomach. He was nervous, because he was presenting a proposal for financing a new housing development project, a first-time undertaking for him.

Tina Jarrett had been the bank manager when David received loans to purchase the lot of land situated on Lakeshore Road in Etobicoke. He'd told

Tina he planned to develop the lot into high-rise apartment blocks. She'd not been completely enthusiastic about the idea; nevertheless, she'd given David the benefit of her doubt. Now, David was facing Tina again—this time with a proposal in hand for loans to put his plan into action.

"Mr. Clark, I must admit, I admire your get-up-and-go attitude. I will present your proposal to the powers that be for consideration and get back to you with an answer as soon as possible."

Tina was polite, she shielded her emotions in the manner she was trained. Her eyes caught the clock on the wall, and considered it was time for her next customer to come in.

"How is the marble mining business in Jamaica doing?" Tina asked David as an exit question.

"My man down there is doing a good job mining the land and running the business," David answered quickly.

Tina rose from her chair and extended a hand to David. "Good luck, Mr. Clark, I'll be in touch with you."

Three years later, a complex of greenish-colored high-rise apartment buildings rose up by the side of a ravine on Lakeshore Road, accessible to major highways with a superb view of Lake Ontario.

David Clark's sweat, together with financing from his banker, had advanced the completion of the enormous residential project known as The Emerald Place.

Situated in The Emerald Place courtyard were three high-rise apartment buildings, each made up of twenty-one floors, known as The Emerald Towers—Tower 1, Tower 2, and Tower 3; and a four-story commercial structure, consisting of small offices, and easily accessible services.

The traffic sign at the turn into The Emerald Place read "No Exit."

By the time Blossom inquired about purchasing a suite the condominiums were sold out.

"We have a three-bedroom suite on the twenty-first floor that was reserved for the developer's family; it is available for rent if you wish to secure it with two months' advance rent," the agent had said.

Blossom did not hesitate. "I'll secure it immediately." she said.

When Blossom entered Suite 2108, she knew she'd found her home—she decided immediately that she would occupy the suite for she knew she could search the area for months and not find a place like The Emerald Towers. Tower 2, Suite 2108, was where she wanted to live.

The suite was large and airy with a marble fireplace, a roomy kitchen, and an enclosed solarium that could be used as a sitting area. The big bay window formed part of the solarium, affording miles and miles of magnificent view. The grounds below were dotted with businesses and bustling activity. Tributary exits from the freeway veered off into roads and streets. And on clear days, Suite 2108 opened up to the stunning outline of the City of Toronto with a remarkable view of the CN Tower. Suite 2108 offered the best—inside and out.

One morning, as Blossom rushed out of the grocery store at the Emerald Place complex to board a streetcar, she bumped into a man carrying a file folder in one hand and a carton of milk in the other. The bump knocked the carton of milk from the man's hand and scattered the contents of his file folder. Embarrassed, she apologized quickly and picked up his scattered papers.

David Clark's real estate offices were on the third floor of the commercial block at the Emerald Place. He was meeting with his project staff that morning and he had stopped in the grocery store to purchase milk for his morning coffee. David handed his project manager the milk and said, "I bumped into a woman at the grocery store and she almost knocked me to the ground." The men laughed at the idea while they poured milk into their coffee.

"She had the biggest, most beautiful bluish–greenish eyes I'd ever seen." David revealed.

"Really?"

"Yes. And she was polite. She apologized when we bumped." David took a long reflective sip from his coffee cup and continued. "She had light brown skin and long black hair. And, did I say she had the biggest, most beautiful bluish–greenish eyes?"

David's project manager eyed him with interest, "You didn't just bump into her, Mr. Clark, you took a good look at her."

"I shouldn't be looking so closely at any woman but my wife," David said candidly. The two men chuckled and then changed the subject to business matters.

David had been absorbed with thoughts about the woman who had bumped him. His imaginings often yielded to her form but he pointedly dismissed the idea of making contact with her as absolutely foolish. *This is crazy, the sort of thing that only occurs in picture shows*, David had said to himself. In his heart, he wished to know the gorgeous woman with bluish–greenish eyes.

David picked up the phone on his desk and dialed the administrator of The Emerald Place Condominium complex.

"Ericka, please make a note to unconditionally renew the rental agreement for the tenant occupying suite 2108 in Building 2."

"Certainly sir," Ericka answered.

FIVE

In the beginning, there was Sheldon.

Sheldon Jason Morgan was a man of worth, although that had not always been the case. He was the only offspring of church leaders and his parents expected him to follow the family tradition and succeed his mother as pastor of the Holiness Church in his hometown just outside of Montego Bay.

When Sheldon quit Manchester Theological College, his mother thought her gospel ministry would decline. His father did not attempt to hide his disappointment and one day he called Sheldon to his side and said: "Son, since you quit theology, then you ought to learn a trade. I'll speak to my friend George Fairweather and see if he'll take you on as an apprentice in his construction business."

Sheldon had attended public school and received further education through college night classes. But nothing could have prepared his parents and those who admired him, for his remarkable success in the earth-moving and construction business.

Sheldon Morgan and Blossom Black first met on a rainy afternoon during a hurricane alert. They'd been students at the same technical institute in Montego Bay.

Everyone had been vigilant in light of the threat of the storm. The weather reports called for extreme conditions and the rains fell nonstop. Traffic lights stayed on red for several hours, and movement was at a standstill.

Schools let out early. People were scrambling to get home as quickly as possible. Blossom hustled through heavy raindrops. She was soaking wet by the time she squeezed into a crammed bus shelter.

Sandwiched between street vendors trying to keep their wares dry, commuters trying to protect themselves from the rain, and students pouring out of the nearby school, Blossom wondered if she would ever get home. She was lucky that her purple plastic raincoat adequately covered her, because her damp dress was already stuck to her body. Suddenly, someone called out, "May I offer you a lift?" Blossom wasn't sure that the question was meant for her, so she looked away, squeezing tightly into one corner of the bus shelter while trying to avoid stepping on someone's toes.

"Miss Black, may I offer you a lift?" she heard someone call out, much louder. She paid attention. Someone whom she did not recognize was beckoning her to come. She moved closer.

"Hop in quickly." He said.

Blossom hopped into an old, banged-up, black Chevrolet van that was sputtering on every drop of gasoline in the tank.

"Hi, my name is Sheldon Morgan … we go to the same school. I know your name is Blossom Black, and you're taking Miss Gordon's business administration classes," he said.

Blossom was glad that Sheldon Morgan knew enough about her to offer her a ride, for she was preoccupied with her uncomfortably damp dress and she was feeling too chilly to try and find a ride on her own.

"How do you like Miss Gordon's classes?" Sheldon asked Blossom in a friendly tone, after she had settled into the passenger seat of his Chevy van.

"I love being in Miss Gordon's classes—I love how she's thorough. I hope she decides to stay to the end of the semester." Blossom felt at ease in Sheldon's company. She continued, "From what I understand, Miss Gordon might move to a college in Kingston. What courses are you taking?" Blossom inquired, glancing sideways at Sheldon.

She noticed his high, well-defined cheekbones and cleft chin; his dark brown skin; his low cut hair and his evenly shaped eyebrows. He was wearing blue jeans and light blue, buttoned-down cotton shirt with the sleeves rolled up to his elbows, showing off his strong forearms. His well-worn work boots had plenty of scuffs and mud marks that made her wonder about his line of work. He bore a certain masculine scent that caught her attention. Blossom noticed a two-way radio mounted on the dashboard and a construction hat and lunchbox resting on the back seat of his vehicle.

"Structural engineering is intense, the course is taking longer to complete because I work and go to school part-time."

"Where do you work?

"Construction. I operate heavy earth-moving equipment on the new highway construction project near Montego Bay. I work for a man named George Fairweather. I have to get my engineering papers, that's why I go to night school." Sheldon's eyes stayed focused on the road ahead.

"Working and going to school part-time is a big responsibility; it requires commitment on your part. How do you do it?" Blossom asked.

"When I dropped out of Bible College, I promised my father I would learn a trade and make something of myself; I believe this course will pay off in the end." Blossom was impressed with Sheldon's commitment to work and school.

Along the way, they conversed about the heavy rainfall, the power outages, and Sheldon's general annoyance with rush-hour traffic.

"I don't like hurricanes; they bring too much rain," Sheldon said, peering between the wiper blades as they moved back and forth across the windshield. The wiper blades suddenly stopped. Sheldon pulled over to the side, hopped out and wiggled the blades to get them started again. He hopped back into his Chevy van.

"Sorry, Miss ... the hardware store sold out of windshield wipers this morning."

Sheldon's good manners appealed to Blossom.

"You can call me Blossom if you'll let me call you ..." her voice trailed off.

Sheldon gave her a soft glance, "Sheldon ... call me Sheldon."

"Sheldon," Blossom paused, "maybe you should stock up on windshield wipers for emergencies like this." She smiled at him.

The weather had gone from bad to worse. Sheldon wiped a hand across the inside of the windshield to clear condensation that had formed. He turned into Blossom's driveway and stopped under the canopy.

"Here Blossom, use this to shield you from the rain," he reached into his glove compartment and pulled out an umbrella that was still in the package.

"Thank you Sheldon."

"You're welcome."

Blossom attempted to open the passenger side door. "Please allow me," Sheldon was poised to open it for her.

When Blossom stepped out of Sheldon's Chevy van, she lost her footing, and landed in his arms. He held her close to steady her and, for a brief moment, their lips met. She pulled away quickly and scooted off to her front door. Sheldon watched as Blossom disappeared into her house.

"The gods are kind to me, even during a hurricane," Sheldon whispered and drove off into the stormy night.

SIX

By the winter of 1985, Blossom Black had already worked eight years at the firm of Johnson, Johnson & Lindsay. Seymour and Ron Johnson had successfully changed over the firm to a combination of family, corporate, and criminal law, staffed with qualified legal professionals.

"Congratulations, on securing the entire commercial portfolio at Acme Logistics, son. Mark Goldberg is a tough nut to crack." Seymour Johnson said to Ron as they took their seats around the boardroom table.

"Thanks Dad ... couldn't let Mark bully me into believing his so-called *extensive* knowledge of corporate law was his trump card."

Father and son chuckled.

Blossom slid a copy of the meeting's agenda across to senior partner, Rupert Lindsay. Rupert glanced at the sheet and put it to the side.

Twenty-five years earlier Rupert Lindsay, Q.C., an experienced patent and trademark attorney and Seymour Johnson, a practicing family law attorney, had formed a successful combination law firm. Now, with his imminent retirement, Rupert was less interested in the goings-on at the firm. He was contented to embrace the fresh thinking of young Ron Johnson and the team of bright lawyers.

Blossom was part of the new breed. Her ambition to succeed was what propelled her to go above and beyond on behalf of the firm and it paid off. Rupert Lindsay taught her the basics of the patent, trademark business, and qualified her to be in charge of that department.

"I am pleased with the administrative changes you've made here, Blossom ... You've simplified our daily operations, and we're satisfied with your performance," Seymour Johnson told Blossom.

She nodded.

When the meeting ended, Ron Johnson requested Blossom to meet with him in his office after lunch.

"Very well, Mr. Johnson," was her reply.

Ron's snap request for a meeting with her was unsettling. The call set her stomach churning. She wondered what she had done that was not up to Ron's standards. Well, if she had made a terrible mistake, then she was prepared to grovel, go down on her knees, and promise she would never let it happen again.

Blossom's assistant, Ruby Snipes, was standing close to the elevators when she exited the boardroom. "May I bring you back some lunch, Miss Black?"

"Tossed salad with croutons, thank you, Ruby."

Blossom was confident in her favorite dark blue Emanuel pantsuit, designed with a Nehru collar. Her hair rested in the curve of her back and the six-inch red pump she wore that day was her most comfortable pair.

After a slight knock, a moment's wait, and his permission to enter, Blossom opened the door to Ron's office and entered.

She turned around to close the door, but Ron was already standing next to her with his hand on the door handle. He closed the door quietly and walked back to his desk. Blossom leaned against the door.

"Have a seat, Miss Black," Ron pointed to the chair in front of his desk. He tilted back in his executive chair with his long legs slightly angled on top of his desk. *He's too relaxed to be serious about anything he's about to say*, Blossom thought.

She sat on the edge of the wide leather chair facing Ron and leaned forward. Her eyes followed his hand movement as he pulled a folder from one corner of his desktop into the center. Her heart sank. *This must be serious*, she thought. Ron noticed her nervousness.

"Relax, Miss Black."

He got up and strode over to his automatic coffee maker and poured two cups.

"Milk and sugar?"

"No, thank you," she answered politely. He smiled at her as he handed her a cup. She took a small sip. It had been her third coffee that morning.

"I'm pleased to see that the trademark for *Beautiful Nails* aesthetics was approved. Good work, Miss Black."

Blossom relaxed her posture. She felt less tension. The hot sip of coffee had generated tiny sweat beads that started to cool her brow.

"*Nails Are Us* fought hard to block *Beautiful Nails'* application for a trademark even though I assured them there would be no chance for a mix-up between the two companies' logos," Blossom explained with much confidence.

Ron smiled, obviously pleased with Blossom's performance in the *Beautiful Nails* matter. He pulled out three pages from the folder on his desk and slid them across to her. She glanced questionably at him.

"Miss Black, it is my pleasure to inform you that the firm appointed you to Office Administrator starting immediately ... This is your letter of appointment." Blossom read the typed sheets.

"A promotion!" she exclaimed.

Ron held out his hand. "Congratulations." His grasp was strong and steady.

"I am very happy Mr. Johnson ...The firm will

not regret it's decision to promote me."

"Please … Call me Ron"

"With pleasure … Ron."

Within minutes of the news about her promotion, Blossom dialed long distance.

"Hello Daddy, guess what … I've just been promoted to Office Administrator of the firm.

"I'm proud of my baby!" Blossom's father exclaimed. "Are you still comfortable in the condo where you're living baby?"

"Oh yes, Daddy … I love this place, the view from the 21st floor is gorgeous," Blossom was excited.

Her father was happy to know that she'd found her niche. He'd hoped his baby girl would return and be close to him, but her future was unfolding in a good way and he was pleased. He accepted that Blossom would most likely not return to live in Montego Bay.

"How is your mini-van running Daddy … good? Does it need spare parts? I'll send you enough money to buy the spare parts you need for your van. And your sax, how is it playing? Does it need a tune up? Daddy, how much money would you like me to send you?" Blossom's excitement bubbled over.

"Be well my little one." her father said before they hung up the phone. He understood it would not be right to accept a financial offering from his daughter. He'd always taken pride in being able to provide for his family and he was determined to let things stay the same. He would say no to her offering.

SEVEN

For Blossom Black, a typical day at the firm involved handling patent and trademark matters, dealing with human resources and personnel affairs, attending to support facilities, and coordinating staff meetings. Today, she's tasked with terminating Aston James the senior accounting officer of the firm, a man whom she'd respected.

Blossom sat back in her chair and waited to be called into the boardroom to carry out the task.

It's unfortunate, she said to herself as she exited the boardroom after terminating Aston. She watched him gather up his papers before she escorted him to get the rest of his belongings.

Blossom sat down with Ruby Snipes to sort through her phone messages. She noticed a message from Jacob, her hair stylist to be at his salon on time if she did not want to be replaced by her physician, Karen Taylor. She couldn't decide whether to fashion her hair in an upsweep or let it fall—either way would be fine, as she always managed to pull off a glamorous look at office get-togethers.

Preparations for the annual Christmas party were already made and all that remained was for Blossom to purchase a gift for someone whom she would be exchanging with—a tradition the firm took seriously.

She had already settled on wearing a full-length, V neck black knit dress with long sleeves and gold accessories.

"That's it," Blossom said and pulled a bunch of keys out of her handbag. She turned to Ruby and said; "Please save my messages until Monday when I'm in again."

"Very well, Miss Black" Ruby was scribbling in her notebook.

Blossom quickly entered an elevator to the lobby and then exited the front door. She stood on the curb for a brief moment and looked around. The atmosphere was overcast, the streets were lightly dusted with snowflakes and people were dashing about in every direction.

Christmas was approaching; shops and homes were already decorated, and ornamental lights flickered around store windows and lamp posts.

Blossom blended into the active crowd, on her way to her hairdresser. She was happy to be out of Jacob's hair salon in an hour.

On her way home, she stopped at the pet food store to get treats for her cat, Fee. She recognized Mr. Mullins, her next-door neighbor. He was walking his terrier Rodney. Mr. Mullins held the dog's leash tightly as it dragged him into a snowy patch of grass to do its business.

By the time Blossom arrived at her apartment, her nose was red and her eyes were wet from walking through blowing snow. The concierge handed her a box marked "Special Delivery." It was wrapped in festive paper with a large red and gold bow on the top. The card read, "Merry Christmas, Bloss—from Sheldon." She smiled and opened the box immediately, dark chocolates, the kind she loved.

She unlocked the front door of her suite, grateful that her walk was only fifteen minutes.

"You ought to thank me for pushing you to rent a place that's only a few blocks from the office," Blossom's colleague Connie always reminded her.

The phone had been ringing. She picked up the one on the kitchen wall.

"Hello?"

"Bloss?"

Her mother was calling.

"Hi, Mom."

"I've been trying to reach you all evening."

"You got me now, Mom."

"Bloss, your father passed early this morning. Try to come home for his funeral."

Her mother hung up.

Blossom stood in the center of her kitchen, stunned. She held the phone for a moment before she placed it back on the hook. Then she picked up the phone again and dialed long distance to her mother—her mother's phone line was busy.

She leaned against the kitchen cabinet and waited for her mother to ring back and finish the conversation, she was not certain if she'd heard her mother correctly. *Did Mom say Daddy had passed?* Blossom asked herself. She wasn't sure if she should begin to cry—yet. All of a sudden she felt mixed up—not sure what to do next. She gathered up her hair, made it into a twist, and headed to the shower, mindful her mother might call back and she might not hear the phone when it rang. As she turned off the shower and reached for a towel to wrap around her body, the phone rang again. She quickly wrapped a smaller towel around her hair and took two steps over to the night table in her bed room.

"Hello Mom."

"Bloss?"

It had been an hour since her mother called. The noise coming through the telephone line was distracting. Blossom pressed the receiver to her ear.

"Yes, Mom?"

"Odette will be helping with the planning of your father's funeral."

Mom, why do you have to ring back two and three times to finish a point when you know this is such a serious matter? She wanted to shout over the phone at her mother, but she kept calm.

"Mom, what did you say when you called before? Did you say Daddy passed?"

"Yes, Bloss ... Three o'clock this morning ... He laid his head in my lap and went to sleep."

More shockwaves rippled through Blossom's body. She put her free hand on her forehead.

"Mom, you're confusing me ... What do you mean when you say, Daddy went to sleep?"

Her mother sighed. "Bloss, you're repeating the same questions to me ... your Daddy died with his head resting in my lap at three this morning ... do you understand that?"

Blossom shook her head vigorously, "Mom ... don't worry...I'll assist Odette with the funeral arrangement and I'll cover the funeral costs."

"Remember to talk to Father George about church stuff." Blossom's mother said and hung up.

Blossom braced herself for more brief phone calls from her mother—no use in trying to prolong her brief conversations.

News about her father's passing presented Blossom with realities she'd been long avoiding; she never expected her father's health to worsen as quickly as it did.

Blossom's pain was the same for her mother. It had not been easy for her mother to deal with her father's illness. Caring for her father had become a tremendous chore for her mother, and toward the end, her mother believed she was the unfortunate wife of a husband who, in her mind, was dying too young. Blossom was upset. She had an urgent desire for a breakfast meal.

"What will you be requiring for dinner this evening Miss Black?" Julia, the waitress at the nearby diner asked Blossom, in her usual chirpy voice. Blossom looked over the Menu list Julia had handed to her then she closed it.

"May I have three scrambled eggs, 2 slices of dry toast, two slices of crispy bacon, a small glass of orange juice and a half cup of coffee?" Blossom asked Julia.

"Sure thing, Miss Black," Julia answered.

Blossom could hold out no longer, she held her head down and burst out into tears for her father.

EIGHT

Whitfield Norman Black, popular saxophone player and leader of the Whitey Black Reggae Band, was an even mix of African and Portuguese ancestry. He was a charming, attractive man with wavy black hair and moustaches that curled at both ends. He was of medium build, stocky, and appeared shorter than his five foot seven. What he lacked in height he made up for in charisma.

This ambitious man from the small town of Downer on the southern side of Jamaica was a brilliant entertainer who wanted to make a big name for himself in the reggae music world. He began to play the saxophone when he was twelve years old at the insistence of his music teacher, and he perfected a unique style that attracted thousands of fans.

His appeal garnered him the attention of the most beautiful women for miles around. They came to hear him play, and they worshiped at his feet in the most extraordinary ways. His charm was not his only charismatic feature—Whitey Black, as he was popularly known, was intelligent, purpose driven, ambitious and poised for greatness.

"I'm easy," Whitey would say before he opened a session. Some people said Whitey Black gave himself too easily when the ladies flung themselves into his arms, and that may have been the reason he'd fathered children outside of his marriage.

Whitey Black married beautiful Margareta Doreen Cassel, a delicate, petite, woman of European ancestry. Margareta looked every inch a dancer: She had a fine-featured oval face, light brown complexion, small hands and feet, flowing blonde hair that fell to the small of her back and beautiful green eyes

Margareta got her first job as an exotic dancer at the Wagon Wheel Night Club when she was seventeen years old—not exactly the place her parents expected their only daughter to begin her dancing career after she'd finished ballet at Alma's School of Dancing.

Margareta's parents weren't rich, but they weren't poor either—they were successful sugar cane farmers—living comfortably.

During the time that Margareta was working at the Wagon Wheel Night Club, a new band called the Whitey Black Reggae Band had a three-month gig at the club. That was when Margareta met and fell in love with the good-looking band leader, Whitfield Black and, for the two of them; it was love at first sight. Not long after that, Margareta found herself with child. Her father insisted that the "son of a gun" marry his daughter or he would give Whitey Black a bloody nose.

"Whitey, you gone and knocked-up the dancer, what's wrong with you, man?" Whitey's friend Melvin Gibson had scolded.

"I love her, man ... I'm going to make her my wife." Whitey had said.

Margareta was in love with Whitey just as she was preoccupied with keeping an eye on him when he was in the company of the ladies, but she never provoked or confronted him in a hostile way. She catered to his every need and accompanied him on his out-of-town gigs. She was determined to make her relationship with Whitey work even though her father had had reservations.

Margareta's obsession with keeping a watchful eye on Whitey had been because of an affair that had developed between Whitey and Gladys Reid, the biological mother of Blossom's half-sister Odette Black.

When Blossom and Odette were old enough, Margareta told the girls—as they were often called—a simple story about beautiful Gladys Reid. Gladys was attending university when Whitey Black played at her graduation dance. Gladys fell in love with Whitey and followed his band for a while. Along the way, Whitey and Gladys Reid coupled. Gladys gave birth to a beautiful baby girl whom Whitey and Margareta adopted and named Odette after Margareta's grandmother.

"Odette is a delightful addition to our family, Whitfield ... and a playmate for Blossom ... Thank heavens for her," Margareta had declared.

Margareta Black was determined to raise her daughters as loving sisters, and although Gladys Reid made several attempts to reclaim her child, Odette would not leave Blossom's side.

As Margareta looked after her daughters, Whitey Black focused on his music career. But things had not been entirely smooth for Whitey.

"Madge honey, my biggest concern is to make sure the instruments are in fine working order. Maybe I should just give up the band and start a chicken farm ... selling chickens and eggs could sustain my family."

"You love the band too much, Whitfield, you'll never give it up ... Besides, you couldn't desert your fans that way ... and anyway, raising chickens is a lot of work that you won't like."

"Honey, the band is costing me too much to maintain, and these days, the guys are demanding more money for each session ... and petrol ... I can hardly afford petrol for my mini-van ..." Margareta had heard enough.

"I'll get a loan from Papa."

"No. No more loans, Madge. Your parents are already paying for extra lessons for our daughters. Honey, no more loans from your parents."

Margareta was content to make do with what monies Whitey gave her as long as he allowed her to travel with the band on his road gigs, yet she was worried about the constant lack of money in the family.

"Maybe I'll help Alma at the dance school. After all, her joints are getting stiff, and she did ask me to help her tutor the students."

"Madge, I know what I'll do. I'll offer each man the opportunity to own his guitar, that way he'll be responsible for its upkeep, that's what I'll do."

"Whitfield, honey, remember you tried that before when you loaned your rhythm guitar to Ainslie Roberts. And what did he do? He quit the band with your guitar, took one of your men with him and formed his own band."

"You're right, Madge some people aren't grateful. Maybe you should help Alma tutor the students at the dance school. That would bring in some needed cash."

"I'll do it, honey."

As time went by, Whitey Black's Reggae Band began to decline, and he took up drinking. His heavy alcohol use caused his health to deteriorate. And, before long, he was confined to Blossom's former bedroom, helpless in the face of liver cancer and surviving the pain with the help of morphine drips.

"You should come home now, Bloss," Whitey Black had advised his daughter over the phone.

"Wait for me Daddy, I'll be home to see you soon," Blossom had assured her father.

"Your mother will need you when I'm gone."

"Daddy, don't talk like that you're scaring me."

"Your Daddy is very ill, Bloss. He's not trying to scare you," Margareta had said.

As Whitey's condition got worse, he and Margareta discussed his funeral arrangement.

"Remember to send mi band suit to the dry cleaners," Whitey instructed Margareta. She assured him she would carry out his final wishes to his satisfaction although she protested his wish to be dressed in his band suit.

"Honey, I will not lay you to rest in that old suit, Bloss will bring with her from Toronto a crisp, new charcoal three-piece suit, befitting the well-known band leader that you are," Margareta had said.

And, for the last time, Whitey Black honored his wife with his familiar, husky laugh.

Back in her suite from her breakfast/dinner at the nearby diner, Blossom stood in her solarium and looked down below; the snow that started earlier grounded highway traffic to a standstill and snowplows and fire trucks struggled for driving room. In her kitchen, she put the kettle on for tea.

Her eyes caught the collage of family photos that hung on the far wall—her parent's wedding picture, her and her sister's baptismal photos, and a picture of her father proudly holding up his sax.

The reality of her father's death was painful. She needed a temporary distraction from her grief, and the firm's Christmas party the next evening would be a perfect diversion.

NINE

LaSalle was a cozy Italian restaurant situated in downtown Toronto at the foot of Bay Street on the shores of Lake Ontario; the perfect location for a Christmas party.

The dining tables at LaSalle were set and beautifully decorated, each having a vase with fresh poinsettias in the center. The chairs were ample and well cushioned. A grand piano was fixed in one corner of the dining room and the pianist played like the inspired entertainer that he was.

Cutlery tinkled against plates and wine glasses clinked in toasts. Lovely ladies swanned around in fitted clothing. Senior Partner, Rupert Lindsay and his wife Donna shared a toast. Staff hobnobbed and shared hugs and kisses. Mark, the courier, was having a laugh with his girlfriend. Wilson from the mailroom was standing at the bar with a drink in his hand. Maggie Langdon, the effervescent, and amusing receptionist, was looking intently into the eyes of a young man at her table. Ruby Snipes was without an escort. Talks turned from whispers to chatter and laughter. Cheerfulness was in the air. Everyone was in a jolly mood.

CEO, Seymour Johnson seemed satisfied with the fine turnout; he removed his spectacles to assess the large gathering.

Blossom's eyes caught Ron Johnson's tall figure leaning against the bar counter in the far corner of the room. He was dressed in formal attire and carelessly sipping from a wine glass. When Ron's eyes met Blossom's he raised a brow. Blossom shifted her gaze in the hope that Ron wouldn't see her connecting eyes as an invitation to come over and join her.

Blossom would not have been bothered by Ron's attention had she not been feeling something special for him. Ron's eligibility as the most qualified unattached man in the firm was no secret, yet Blossom never admitted she was charmed by his good looks and appeal.

"Isn't he marvelous? He goes home regularly to have dinner with his mother." Ruby Snipes had openly disclosed, one afternoon, when the three of them had been standing at the water cooler. Blossom recalled the flush she felt in her cheeks, and how bashful Ron looked when Ruby made the pronouncement. Ruby's decorum was clearly off-kilter that afternoon.

Suddenly, Blossom remembered an encounter with Ron that had caught her off-guard. The two of them had been in the filing room pouring over confidential records and documents to be entered into evidence in an upcoming trademark proceeding. She was wrapped up in the activity, with her lips slightly parted and her head somewhat tilted. All of a sudden, she felt Ron lips pressing against hers. She was surprised.

Puzzled by his forwardness Blossom closed the file cabinet immediately and said, "Mr. Johnson, I do not appreciate what you just did, is this the way you treat your female employees?" And she turned and walked toward the door of the filing room.

Ron leaned against the door to keep it shut. "Please forgive me, Miss Black," he said, "I acted like a jerk. What I did is not how I normally treat female employees in this firm. You are a beautiful woman, I intended to compliment you and I went too far…I'm truly sorry." Blossom accepted Ron's apology although his kiss had left a question in her mind that she was not prepared to answer.

"Nice, isn't it?" Ron had moved to where Blossom was standing in the ballroom at LaSalle. He was pointing to the beautifully adorned Christmas tree.

"Lovely tree," Blossom nodded and accepted the

glass of wine Ron placed in her hand. He touched her fingers lightly as he let go of the wine glass. Blossom excused herself and walked toward the big glass door that led out to the patio—she needed fresh air.

The night was cool. Sharp gusts from the lake pushed a lock of hair against her ear; she inhaled deeply. When she turned around she saw Ron close behind. His being there didn't matter.

"You look stunning," Ron said, bringing his drink to his lips. His eyes never left hers.

"Thank you, Ron. You look pretty handsome yourself," she tried hard not to be overly flattering.

Blossom watched as Ron's eyes dropped down the full length of her body. He certainly knew how to compliment a woman without saying much. He came closer and put an arm around her.

It felt good. She didn't resist him.

She remained still and enjoyed the moment.

With his hand touching her, she could endure the pain she was feeling about her father's passing.

Blossom's thoughts soared to other Christmases. In her hometown, twenty-six miles east of Kingston, Blossom Black's family traditionally gathered at the home of her grandmother, for hot cocoa, just before everyone trotted off to the nearby Anglican Church for Christmas morning service.

Grandma Black always insisted that the family be in church very early on Christmas morning to be certain that they got their usual seats.

"We don't want the folks who only come to church on Christmas day occupying our seats, do we?" Grandma Black always said.

The gathering at Grandma Black's dining table after church was a big event; she was happy when the entire family came for Christmas dinner and especially cheerful when her musician son Whitfield and her daughter-in-law Margareta, whom she affectionately named Madge, showed up.

When it was time to say grace, everyone at the dining table avoided Grandma Black's eyes so as not to be called upon to do the honors.

"We ought to give thanks for the meal we're about to eat …" Grandma Black announced and her eyes settled on Odette.

"Odette, please say the Christmas grace." said Grandma Black. Odette habitually protested.

"I don't want to say grace, Grandmother … Bloss, you say grace." Odette looked at Blossom.

Grandma Black knew that Odette and Blossom would argue about who should say grace until the meal turned cold, so she usually broke out into grace, ending with "… and Lord, why does Odette always gets her own way?"

The family typically settled down to a meal of roasted pig; goat meat curry; steamed rice made with coconut milk and red kidney beans; roasted sweet potatoes; sweet white yams; fried ripe plantains; black pudding, and Grandma Black's festive red drink.

After dinner, the whole family, as a rule, dashed over to Grandma Black's rocking chair in the vestibule where the presents piled high. Christmas wrapping paper would be unceremoniously ripped and boxes sent flying to the delight of everyone.

"A Penny for your thoughts Blossom," Ron said.

"I'm sorry Ron; I was preoccupied with family matters."

"Would you like to tell me about it?" He asked.

"No, thank you Ron ... Maybe tomorrow."

Blossom studied Ron's silhouette. His neatly trimmed moustaches were what she found most attractive. She'd always admired the comical way he cocked his brow and his playful winks at her to show his approval.

Tonight I'll be less concerned about his behavior, I'll relish his attention, Blossom thought as she let Ron trail his fingers down to the ridge at her lower back.

She remembered how taken aback she'd been the time when he'd shown his admiration and she would not overreact this time. He remembered her reaction the time he'd shown his admiration and he didn't want to be ill-mannered. Neither of them wanted to make a serious move. He could not read her thoughts, and she could not guess his; they were brooding over their feelings. He spoke first.

"Let's go back inside."

The Christmas party was swinging. A disc jockey had taken over from where the pianist had left off, and the dance music had become soulful.

"Happy Holidays, Miss Black," Connie sounded out, when she recognized Blossom entering the ballroom. The holiday greeting from Connie might have been an invitation for Blossom to come and join the ladies at Connie's table. Ron turned to face Blossom, "May I have this dance?" he said. Blossom slid into Ron's arms, ready to re-experience the sensations she'd had with him minutes earlier.

With his hands curved around her waist and with hers on his shoulders, they danced to several songs. Blossom hoped that no one took special notice she'd been dancing several sets with the son of the head honcho of the firm. Slow songs gave way to ones with faster tempos. Ron pretended not to notice and continued his slow rhythm. Blossom yielded to Ron's movements.

Suddenly, she felt a strong pulse from Ron's thighs. She gasped. Her knit dress provided no barrier for the heat that was coming from Ron's expensive suit pants. She pulled back.

"I'm sorry," he said.

Ron's loin was on fire, and he was willing to let it burn—his body did not feel like that of a man who was sorry for what was happening.

The fiery exchange left Ron and Blossom looking like guilty puppies. It was taking him a while for his emotions to subside. Blossom pressed into his loin to cover his raw desire and he was grateful for her understanding. He looked at Blossom with a bashful smile and said, "I ought to take responsibility for what just happened ... although I know that no average man can resist your attraction."

Blossom remained silent.

She was not ready to turn back on years of dismissing Ron and suddenly see him as a boyfriend. Perhaps it was the simple matter of a glass of wine having gone much farther than to their heads. Deep down, Blossom knew she'd been developing a strong likeness for Ron; and there was little doubt about Ron's physical need for her—the reaction from his loin said everything. People started to leave the Christmas party.

"May I escort you home?" Ron asked, guiding Blossom to the door of LaSalle.

She thought it might not be a good idea to be alone with Ron. *Heck no, considering how we rattled each other's nerves on the dance floor,* Blossom wanted to say. Instead, she touched the lapel of his overcoat and said, "Thank you Ron, I'll be fine."

Ron put an arm around her shoulder, "I'm pleased with the work of your staff in pulling together a successful Christmas party, but something is worrying you, what is it Blossom?"

"I will admit to you Ron ... I received word from my mother yesterday that my father passed. I will be off to Montego Bay the end of the week."

"I'm very sorry to hear about your father,

Blossom, take as much time off as you need."

"Thank you, I appreciate your thoughtfulness."

Ron kissed her lightly on the cheek, "If there is something else I can do for you in your time of grief please let me know."

Blossom nodded.

They stepped out into the cool, crisp December night. "Taxi!" Blossom called out.

"Where to, ma'am?" the cab driver asked.

"The Emerald Place, Tower 2," she answered.

Blossom settled into the back seat of the cab, grateful that the traffic lights were cooperating. She opened the window and inhaled cool air.

"You've reached your destination, ma'am."

The cab driver opened the rear door. Blossom paid the fare and hurried into her lobby.

"Hello Miss Black," the concierge came out of his cubicle and he handed her a stack of mail. "Your mailbox was full, ma'am."

"Thank you, Freddie."

She walked into an open elevator, going up. The flickering red light on her phone, when she entered her suite, indicated she had messages. Blossom checked—her mother had called several times. She knew her mother needed to be consoled, but it was too late to return her mother's call. Blossom made a journal entry.

December 18: I love you, Mom, and I loved Daddy too, I wish I was with you right now, but too many miles separate us—goodnight, Mom.

TEN

The chiming intercom sounded like a fire alarm bell. She threw her aching head back on the pillow. "Concierge, Miss Black ... The airport limousine is here for you."

"I'll be down in fifteen minutes, Freddie."

Blossom leaped out of bed and rushed to the shower. She would be late getting to the airport if she didn't leave quickly and if she got caught in rush-hour traffic, her *goose is cooked*.

Blossom packed some things in her carry-on bag and then dressed quickly. She looked at her appearance in the hallway mirror before she walked hurriedly to the elevators going down. Heavy winds coming off Lake Ontario hit Blossom's face as she stepped out into the morning. The cold wind penetrated her overcoat. She shivered and tucked her scarf under her collar. Snow accumulation that had banked up on the sidewalk the night before made it difficult for the airport limousine to get close to the curb.

"I can help you over the snowbank, Miss Black," Freddie offered.

"Thanks Freddie." Blossom said and accepted his hand.

The limousine bumped its way out to the main road and merged onto the freeway.

Snow-removal equipment on Highway 401 brought traffic to a standstill. Blossom looked at her wristwatch; she was nervous that she might not make it to the airport on time.

"What terminal?" the limo driver asked.

"Terminal 2."

"You're going south?"

"Yes."

She did not want to encourage small talk; her main concern was getting to Pearson Airport on time. The drive was bumper-to-bumper, she would be lucky if the limo driver dropped her off at Departures in less than an hour.

Terminal 2 was buzzing with activity at 7:15 a.m. People were checking their luggage, bidding farewells, having a second cup of coffee and *killing* time. There were several announcements about planes that were being de-iced. The flight to Montego Bay was already running late. Snow was coming down in larger, heavier flakes with no sign of letting up.

The smell of fresh coffee excited Blossom's senses. She ordered a small coffee from the coffee stand and sat at the counter. She recognized a *National Geographic* magazine on the newsstand. The picture of a cat on the front cover reminded her of her cat Fee. She was glad that Mrs. Mullins, her next-door neighbor, had volunteered to take care of Fee while she was away.

There was plenty happening in the airport lounge to distract Blossom from her anxieties. "Paging Blossom Black ... Blossom Black, please pick up the nearest wall telephone."

Blossom picked up a phone, "Hello?"

Ron Johnson was at the other end. "Hello, Blossom ... Ron here ... Ruby told me you're on your way to Montego Bay for your father's funeral I want to wish you a safe journey. Remember to take as much time off as you need and let me know if there's anything more I can do for you."

"Thanks a lot, Ron, I'll only be away ten days."

"Goodbye then ... Travel safely."

Blossom had not said much about her father's passing to anyone at the firm, and she had only told her assistant, Ruby Snipes, about her trip to Montego Bay. Dear, sweet Ruby—by no means a gossip—a lovely person who only gave information to the people who mattered. Blossom dialed Ruby with last minute instructions. "Hello, Ruby, this is Miss Black ... Mr. Johnson's presentation material for his two o'clock meeting at the Harbor Castle Convention Centre is on his desk … in the black leather folder … next to the folder from accounting. Please bring it to his attention?"

"Very well, Miss Black."

"Thank you, Ruby," she ended the call.

"Flight 225 to Montego Bay now boarding …" came the announcement from the overhead public address system.

Blossom picked up her carry-on bag and clutch purse and headed toward the boarding door. People were hurrying to get on board. She claimed her seat by a window and looked outside at the gray skies and wet, flaky snow then she pulled down the shades.

Blossom requested the attendant to let her sleep for an hour and then sank into her seat for a long nap. She was delighted when she pushed up the shades later and saw clear blue skies and fluffy white clouds. As it turned out, a long nap was the antidote to any fears she may have had concerning the weather and its emotional impact on her psyche. She noticed that the headache she had been nursing was gone.

The attendant leaned into Blossom's seat and said.

"Ma'am … coffee or tea?"

Blossom considered another cup of coffee and then changed her mind.

"May I have something stronger than coffee?" she asked. The woman seated beside Blossom turned a puzzled look. Blossom acknowledged her gaze, "I'm grieving for my father," she disclosed.

"I'm sorry for your pain," the woman said and left her alone.

It was tough for Blossom to grasp that she would never hear her father speak again. Sadness overtook her as memories of him cascaded through her thoughts, but she would have plenty of time to reflect on his passing before the plane landed.

On arrival in Montego Bay, Blossom made her way through the busy airport to await her ride. She remembered the funeral director saying the heavy rain they'd been experiencing might delay her father's funeral plans. Delays aside, Blossom's hope was that when everything was all said and done, her father would have had the best sendoff—ever.

ELEVEN

Whitey Black's funeral would be a family event. Blossom's Aunt Lucille and her daughter Jennie would be arriving from New Jersey; her Uncle Granville from Florida and her Aunts Christie and Eulalee from Sheffield, England. Blossom's 94-year-old great aunt, Nana Mae Black, whom Blossom was named after and who she was so much looking forward to seeing again, insisted on making the trip from New York. Blossom's cousin Darlene and her husband Clinton would be arriving from Toronto with their three-year-old daughter Riley.

"You want to make a phone call, ma'am?" A man was pointing to a phone booth across the street. Blossom was about to reply to him when she heard someone shouted, "Bloss ... over here!"

Blossom sighed in relief at the sound of her sister, Odette's voice coming from a Honda automobile. She pulled her luggage to Odette's parked car. "You drive a nice car, Odie," Blossom said and hopped into the front seat.

"Thanks Bloss. It's a gift from hubby, Winston."

"How has he been keeping? How has his commuter plane business been doing?

"His passenger planes fly twice a week from Montego Bay to Kingston ... he's looking to put in an additional trip to accommodate the increase in passenger ridership."

"Very nice, Odie ... I'm proud of Winston."

Blossom was certain that Odette had lots of news to share and if there were blanks, Margareta Black would fill them in with embellishments.

Odette had worked alongside the funeral directors to finalize their father's preparations.

"Mom told me you handled the nuts and bolts of Daddy's funeral very well. You took a big burden off Mom's shoulders, Odie."

"Yes, and you did too Bloss, you took care of the finances. Daddy's Life Insurance wouldn't have been sufficient to afford him the sendoff he'll be getting. We loved Daddy, he's worthy of our best."

Blossom lay back in the passenger seat and closed her eyes.

Odette made the turned onto the long driveway that led to her beautiful stucco decorated home, "Wake up Bloss, we're home."

* * *

The evening sun dropped behind the Blue Mountain, and night lights started to come on. Blossom reclined on Odette's back porch wearing a floral cotton skirt neatly tucked between her legs to shield her from inquisitive eyes that might be lurking between bamboo trees. She watched as bamboo stalks moved backward and forward, with just enough sway to let the dim distant lights come through. She was ready to kick back and relax when Odette called out.

"Bloss ... telephone!"

Odette stood on the inside of her kitchen door holding a phone out to Blossom.

"Who is it?"

"Someone you know ... Take the call."

Blossom took the phone.

"Hello, this is Blossom?"

"Hi, Bloss; you arrived safely."

"Sheldon! How did you know I was here?"

"Your mother told me you'd be home ... and anyway," Sheldon paused, "how could you not be home for your father's funeral?"

"Yes, yes, you're right, Sheldon, I had been meaning to phone you before I arrived ... had a lot on my mind."

"I understand let's have dinner at Cool Runnings?"

"Okay. What time?"

"Eight?"

"See you then."

Blossom handed the phone back to Odette and scampered inside. She quickly surveyed Odette's walk-in closet and pulled out a pair of size 9 designer jeans and a t-shirt that said "One Love" on the front. The jeans hugged Blossom's form as though they were her own. She walked into the kitchen where Odette was pouring ice tea in tall glasses.

"Perfect," Odette exclaimed, when she looked her sister up and down.

Sheldon knocked at Odette's door at precisely seven o'clock. Blossom opened the door.

"Hi, Sheldon," she said and ran to him.

Sheldon held her at arm's length and looked at her admiringly. She noticed a look that said "wow" and waited to hear Sheldon say the word. The pause was long. "There is something the matter?" Blossom inquired with some concern.

"No, no, nothing's the matter, Bloss … It's your beautiful shape that I see."

"My shape is the same as when you saw me six months ago, Sheldon," Blossom said, "and the times before …" she trailed off, smiling.

"Bloss, you have not changed," Sheldon said with a broad smile. He kissed her on the lips. "Your beauty is matchless."

Sheldon was casual in cotton shirt, blue jeans, running shoes, and a ball cap. He took her hand and guided her to his car.

They drove off to Cool Runnings, a quaint little restaurant at the tip of an adjoining town.

As they made their way along the narrow road, Blossom thought back to when she and her friends had walked two miles every Sunday after mass to go to the Holiness Church pastored by Sheldon's mother, mainly to see the cool "holy ghost" boys who went to that church.

"How have things been since we last saw each other, your business, your mother, your mother's church?" Blossom asked.

"You remember Pastor Mackie? ... Pastor Mackie is now doing the bulk of the ministry work." Sheldon informed Blossom.

"Good ... and Mother Morgan?"

"Mother is mostly doing paperwork for the church ... Dad's dementia turned into full-blown Alzheimer's disease and mother hired someone to be with him when she can't be at home."

"Sorry to hear about your father, Sheldon. How has Mr. Fairweather been keeping?"

"Fairweather stays at home since his retirement, he and I meet occasionally for light conversations. He advised me to hire a competent project manager to assist me and I did, his name is Michael Dixon. Together, we coordinate the earthmoving contracts."

"Mr. Fairweather had employed some experienced men, as I recall," Blossom said.

"Most definitely. I had to pension off some of the old men and hire younger men who're able to do lifting and moving with heavy equipment. I even hired a few of Wilbrothers Construction men ... the ones who were laid off after their labor dispute." Sheldon made the turn toward Cool Runnings.

"Why were Wilbrothers men disputing?" Blossom was curious.

"Job security and benefits. Island Workers Union is negotiating with Wilbrothers for a new contract. The atmosphere is tense around here, Doug Williams thinks our company is getting most, if not all, of the new contracts and he is not happy," Sheldon chuckled.

"That's wonderful!"

"I work twenty-four hours a day, seven days a week, Bloss. If I had a wife, I would think twice before I put in so many extra hours." He looked sideways at Blossom and blew her a kiss as he parked his SUV.

When they were last at Cool Runnings, it was dilapidated and shrouded in thick bushes. Now, it looked like the place had been renovated. Blossom noticed steps that led up to the rooftop's dimly lit patio. The dancehall flooring had been widened, and the bandstand had been rearranged for better visibility. The dining room was comfy with smaller, more intimate dining tables and well-padded chairs.

"They improved the place," Blossom observed.

"Good job," Sheldon said, pointing to pictures and paintings on the wall.

In years gone by, when Whitey Black played every Friday and Saturday night at Cool Runnings, the place was rocking. Blossom used to sit on her mother's lap as her father jammed with the band.

"Had to hire two new members and change to a modern reggae beat," Whitey had said to Blossom when she had inquired about how the band was doing.

"New reggae is what the younger generation wants to hear ... had to change with the times" he told her.

When Whitey Black became ill, Melvin Gibson, the drummer in Whitey's band, took over as leader and played exclusively at Cool Runnings.

Sheldon selected a table by the window at the far corner of the dining room. "Hungry?" he asked Blossom.

"I am famished"

"Let's eat then."

From the buffet table, Blossom and Sheldon selected a curry meat dish, steamed white rice, sweet potatoes, and steamed vegetables.

"Peace, Bredda Sheldon," a male voice said as Sheldon and Blossom sat down to eat.

"How's business, Mel?" Sheldon asked without looking up from his meal.

"I man ... seen betta days, Bredda Sheldon," the man Sheldon called Mel answered. He looked at Blossom with squinted eyes. "Mi kno dis lady?" he asked. Blossom looked up and smiled. Melvin recognized her.

"Whitey B dawta from Taranta," he exclaimed. Blossom stood up and threw her arms around Melvin.

"Uncle Sexy, how have you been?" Blossom asked.

"Likkle One ... yu come?"

Likkle One was the name all the members of Whitey Black's Reggae Band called Blossom, when she was growing up. Melvin Gibson was pleased to see that Blossom had made the trip from Toronto to be at her father's funeral.

"Yu fada was not happy dat di new membas af di ban play new reggae ...Whitey B always waan fi keep di ole time beat." Melvin was apologetic.

Blossom sighed.

Melvin Gibson looked much older and probably not as sexy; nonetheless, he'd aged better than the two remaining original band members.

"I goin' mis Whitey B, bad, bad," Melvin said.

Blossom shuddered and Melvin left her alone.

After dinner, Sheldon invited Blossom to sit with him on the rooftop patio. He put his arms around her and blew warm breath through her hair. Blossom nestled against him. Soft moonlight rays cast a shadow of the two of them on the far wall.

"I'm sorry about Whitey. I know he loved you."

"And I loved him too, Sheldon. I'll miss Daddy."

Sheldon gently squeezed Blossom against him.

"How can I comfort you Bloss?" He asked.

Blossom pressed into him and inhaled his scent.

"Just being here with me is what I ask of you Sheldon." Sheldon dominated Blossom's senses whether she was next to him or thousands of miles across the ocean. She placed her hands on the rise in his lap and he made a tender, sensual sound that raised her desire for him. He shifted. His entire body was on fire. She slowly released his firmness from its constraint and his tremors vibrated against her fingers.

"Bloss, will you marry me?" Sheldon asked her.

Blossom was silent.

"Bloss, will you marry me?" Sheldon repeated.

Blossom's heart began to beat faster.

"Give me more time, Sheldon," she answered.

Blossom knew Sheldon would want an answer before she returned to Toronto. He never missed an opportunity to remind her that her rightful place should be by his side, she shivered, Sheldon pressed her to him.

"Bloss ... I'm a man, my needs are great ... It is not my intention to have a fling with another woman ... I love you; marry me and stay here with me. I cannot stand the separation you put me through ... It is painful, it is literally killing me ... You ask me for more time? How much time is more time?" The resoluteness of Sheldon's tone was telling.

Blossom thought for a moment. It is true, her time at the firm had brought her into a close but secretive relationship with Ron Johnson and she had gone to great lengths to keep it that way. She had weighed the pros and cons of breaking up with Sheldon, nonetheless, she carried on a relationship with both men. This might be the moment to come clean about her Toronto affair. In her heart, she knew it was time to be truthful. She ought to terminate her relationship with one of these men. She loved Sheldon, she wanted him in her life and yet she continued to stall her relationship with him even if, in the end, she could lose both men. She shivered. Sheldon felt her shivers. "What's the matter, Bloss?"

"Don't be angry with me because of my wavering Sheldon, I love you … I merely want to be sure of your love."

"Bloss … My love … How can I be angry with you when I love you so much? You can be sure of my love…I love you now and I will love you then. Your absence from my life makes me yearn for you. I'll wait for you … I *will*."

Sheldon could not contain his desire; his lips met hers in a passionate kiss.

The drive back to Odette's place was slow, partly due to the slick road from an earlier drizzle but mostly because Sheldon was thinking about the dilemma in which he had found himself. He'd been dating Maureen Grant, a friend of Blossom and when Maureen proposed marriage he hesitated.

"I love you too Maureen … then again, I must be practical, my business just started to grow and it needs my full attention, having a family now could be a distraction. I cannot be distracted … not yet."

Sheldon bit into his lower lip in frustration. He carefully made the turn on Odette's driveway to avoid any chance of a skid and parked under the canopy.

"Goodnight, my love" he said and leaned over and kissed Blossom. She snuggled closer.

"Stay with me tonight," Blossom whispered.

Sheldon could not resist her request.

"I'll stay with you, Bloss."

Soft raindrops pattered against the car window as they reclined together.

TWELVE

Day broke. Roosters crowed with gusto, and dogs barked as if strangers were in their midst. The smell of clean damp earth stimulated the nostrils, and neighborhood cooking aroused pleasant sensations surpassed only by authentic tastes—the atmosphere was alive.

Blossom let out a sneeze that stirred her senses. She felt strong arms holding her. She turned her face upward and recognized Sheldon looking at her. She laid-back against his chest and yawned, and stretched to his delight.

"Good morning my love, did you sleep well?" Sheldon asked Blossom in a soft voice as he shifted in his seat to relax the noticeable morning rise that had popped up in his lap to greet her. Blossom smiled. "I slept very well."

Suddenly, there was a succession of quick taps on the car window. "Wake up, sleepy heads." Odette announced, holding two mugs of hot chocolate.

The day of Whitey Black's funeral had arrived. Rain had been falling steadily all through the night. Gutters were full and overflowing, grass was soggy and mud was soft—it was a day to wear rain boots.

Cabs and cars, trucks and buses—all forms of transportation pulled up to let off passengers in front of St. Paul's Anglican Church. Mourners scurried into a huge makeshift shelter that had been built in the churchyard to accommodate the overflow. Blossom watched as Odette checked inside the tent to be sure that volunteers were doing what they were supposed to. She was glad that Odette had taken care of various tasks associated with organizing the funeral. *Daddy would have been proud of Odette*, Blossom thought.

Blossom and Odette inched their way to the church entrance. They reached their seats in a front-row pew when Gladys Reid stepped out ahead of them. Gladys's lips moved. Odette pretended not to notice. Blossom was not put off by Gladys' appearance at her father's funeral. She imagined many of her father's lady fans would attend, although she was surprised Gladys Reid had bothered to show up. Gladys was eyeing a seat in the front pew.

"Those seats are reserved for children and relatives of the deceased," a church usher whispered to Gladys. Blossom and Odette waited to be seated. Gladys came close to Blossom and Odette, she appeared anxious, "Don't ignore me, Odette; I will always be your mother," Gladys said, she was looking directly at Odette.

"Keep her away from me," Odette said in an audible whisper.

"Get over it, Gladys." Margareta Black said glaring coldly at Gladys. She had appeared from nowhere and stood between Blossom and Odette.

"All the seats in the front rows are reserved for family, Gladys," Blossom repeated as Gladys tried to seat herself.

"If my daughter is family, so am I," Gladys said, looking directly at Odette.

"I am not your daughter," Odette whispered, loud enough for Gladys to hear.

Terrified that the situation might be developing into an out-of-control scene, Blossom interjected. "Have a seat, Gladys," and pointed her to a seat at the end of the front pew.

The minor fracas died down quickly. Family, relatives and friends settled in their seats. Blossom and Odette were seated in a pew overlooking their father's closed coffin. On top of the coffin was a plaque shaped like a saxophone with the words: *Play On, Whitey Black* written in gold.

The organ piped and mass started. Father George and his entourage marched up the aisle. Kenneth Brown, the acolyte who had carried the cross for a number of years, looked a lot older. He was walking behind a younger, stronger acolyte who was carrying the cross.

Blossom remembered having a crush on Kenneth Brown, when she was fourteen. She remembered how horrified she had been when Father George had announced the engagement of Kenneth Lloyd Brown and Penelope Ann Green.

Odette's hand in hers jolted Blossom, and when she turned to look, she saw that Odette had been crying.

"You're going to be okay," Blossom tried to assure her sister.

"Yes, yes, I know … It's a habit … I always cry at funerals." Odette dabbed her eyes.

Church was packed and overflowing. The air inside was hot. Overhead cooling fans that were usually adequate to cool the packed church struggled to cope with heat generated by hundreds of people inside. Whitey Black's funeral agendas turned out to be handy paper fans for those who were overwhelmed by the hot air. The people who were crammed inside the adjacent tent complained that they could not see or hear what was taking place inside the chapel. It would have been chaotic if Sheldon had not been keeping order.

The church choir began to sing a jazzy version of *Swing Low, Sweet Chariot*. It was difficult to tell whether people were wiping perspiration or drying tears.

Blossom studied the choir; some old, familiar faces were still singing. Penelope Green, her former Grade three teacher, looked healthy and strong, although her hair was completely white. Dorothy Grant sat beside her daughter, Maureen Grant. Mrs. Grant looked somewhat shaky; poor Mrs. Grant, she never bounced back after her husband had died even though Maureen, the town's librarian, still lived at home with her.

Blossom looked over to where Margareta Black was sitting. Her mother's black lace head covering was pulled over her entire face, and she was leaning against Blossom's great-aunt, Nana Mae. Blossom could see that her mother was sniffling into her white lace handkerchief.

Blossom turned and looked at Gladys Reid at the end of her pew; her wide-brimmed hat covered her face and shielded any obvious expression. Both of Gladys's palms were clasped in her lap.

Sheldon's mother marched up to the rostrum outfitted in ceremonial attire and matching headdress. She sat in a high back chair, next to Father George.

Whitey Black's Reggae Band entered the Church in their usual band outfit. They played a rendition of Bob Marley's song: *No, Woman, No Cry*.

Petula McCann came to the microphone. She settled in her usual stance at the lectern and sang *Amazing Grace*. Aunty Tula, as Blossom called her, was one of the original singers in Whitey Black's Band.

Kenneth Brown made his way to the podium to eulogize Whitey Black. He pulled out a white handkerchief from one of his tunic sleeves and passed it over his nose; then he inclined his head toward

Whitey's casket.

"Whitey will be blowing his horn up there ..." Mr. Brown began, his right index finger pointed upward.

Mass was over in an hour, mourners congregated at the church's burial site for Whitey's interment. Silent sniffles and tear-filled eyes were part of the general scene. Some people threw handfuls of earth and others tossed roses on Whitey's casket as it was lowered into the ground. And still, others just waved goodbye. Blossom, though sad, was pleased with the adulation her father's fans had shown.

All of a sudden, a shrill sound pierced the air like a siren; Blossom looked in the direction of the sound. It was difficult to see what was happening, though she recognized her mother in a group that stood off to the side. Both of her mother's hands were flailing in the air, and her head turned upward. Her mother was bawling. Blossom panicked.

"What on earth..." Blossom's voice trailed off. She dashed through the crowd to her mother's side. "What's the matter Mom?" Blossom asked, obviously concerned. Margareta Black shook her head from side to side. Blossom noticed a well-dressed man standing next to her mother. He held up a black umbrella with one hand and his other hand touched her mother's shoulder. The man was a spitting image of her father—could've passed as a blood son. Blossom was confused. Had she not previously identified her deceased father's body, she would've thought this was all a game and Whitey had been alive all along. The man turned around to recognize Blossom; she felt a connection to him, as if they were related. She wasn't sure if she should say something. Her mother was overcome with emotion. Everyone was quiet, although farther out, the burial service continued. The silence was uncomfortably long.

"Boyd Stephenson ... your half-brother from Cleveland, Ohio," the man said.

He seemed composed.

Blossom looked Boyd Stephenson up and down. His expensive suit indicated a man of means and the band on his ring finger was telling.

"Cleveland, Ohio," Blossom repeated to be sure that she had heard him correctly.

How it is that daddy had a son in Cleveland, Ohio? Blossom said to herself. She looked at her mother with questioning eyes. Boyd Stephenson's cool, calm and collected manner intimidated her.

"... And you are a son of my father?

"So my mother told me ... my mother is a honest woman."

"How did you get to Cleveland?"

"After I graduated from law school, I got a job in the legal department at City Hall in Cleveland." Boyd held out his hand. "Delighted to meet you at last, sis." Blossom stretched out her hand to shake Boyd Stephenson's then she pulled her hand back.

"Where did you live before Cleveland?" Blossom asked, still curious.

"Queens, New York—mother traveled with me from Ocho Rios when I was three years old; we lived with my grandmother in Queens."

Blossom was surprised that no one in these parts knew about Boyd Stephenson.

Margareta Black began to talk; "I knew his mother, she was a singer in your father's band."

"You knew about this Mom?" Blossom looked at her in disbelief and embarrassment.

"I knew his mother," Margareta Black repeated. "I did not know she had a son with Whitfield."

Boyd Stephenson hung down his head.

Petula McCann belted out her rendition of the song, *Many Rivers to Cross*. She dragged out the musical notes of the song on a mournful chord. Odette rushed over to Blossom's side, seemingly in a state of anxiety.

"What's going on, Bloss?"

Blossom turned around to face Boyd Stephenson.

"Mr. Boyd Stephenson, meet your sister, Odette Black."

Boyd nodded and shook Odette's hand.

Blossom thought back to when she and Odette were children. Odette might have been disappointed to know that her father had been a married man when he expected her with Gladys Reid, but Odette was fine with the details when they came to light. Odette adored Whitey Black and she and Blossom grew up as loving sisters. *It should have been the same with Boyd Stephenson*, Blossom thought.

* * *

Whitey Black's three children joined hands at his graveside. They watched the last sprinklings of dust being scattered on their father's vault. Grave workers applied the finishing touches and secured a memorial stone that read: *Whitfield Norman Black, August 3, 1926 – December 17, 1985.*

Boyd Stephenson stood between Blossom and Odette with his arms looped into theirs. "I did not know my father the way a son should know his father, all I had were newspaper clippings and photographs of him. I cherished every scrap of information I could find about Father. I'm here today to pay my respects," he said.

"We appreciate the gesture," Blossom said.

Boyd hesitated.

"Can we talk?" He pointed toward a shaded area at the entrance of the cemetery.

Boyd gazed at the vast expanse of the cemetery and began to talk; "I'm glad to have met you both. I admit, I had known about my father's two daughters. I despised the two of you for having him all to yourselves. I always believed that because of you, my father abandoned my mother and me, and forced us to live in the shadows. My father never acknowledged me. He'd only seen me once when I was a young child of three and once in my teenage years when my mother and I visited my great-aunt in Ocho Rios. My mother ... she'd been both mother and father to me while she waited for Father to own me. For reasons not yet known to me, I loved my father. I wanted to make something of myself, to show my father I existed, to make him see that I'm not the throwaway kid he made with my mother many years ago. When I graduated from law school, I phoned to tell Father about my accomplishment. He was too busy to speak to me. He's gone now ..." Boyd deliberated. "My anger over not having my father is over; I have come to terms with my existence." He dabbed his eyes.

Blossom wasn't sure she believed every word that Boyd Stephenson had said but she gave him the benefit of her doubt.

All of a sudden she understood why her mother had always spied on her father—her mother didn't trust her father when he was in the company of other women. Mournful tears for her father welled-up in her eyes and spilled over.

The skies had suddenly become overcast; Boyd turned and looked at Blossom, then at Odette.

"Let's keep in touch," he said and then he walked toward his rental car.

Blossom and Odette returned to where their mother had been standing. Blossom buried her head in her mother's shoulder and cried.

It was a painful day for all but mainly for Blossom. She cried a lot because she'd been missing her father but mostly because she'd been embarrassed by the under current that manifested at her father's interment. It had been a peculiar day.

THIRTEEN

A light drizzle had started and by the time people gathered on Margareta Black's back porch for Whitey Black's reception it had become a downpour. But the rain did not dampen the spirits of the large gathering. Blossom's mother let loose with some of her dance moves and the whole time Blossom held her breath in fear that her mother might fall and injure herself. The crowd jammed to the music of Whitey Black's Reggae Band for hours before anyone took pity on the family and left them alone.

Blossom studied the face of Boyd Stephenson. She imagined she owed him an apology. After all, she and her sister Odette was the recipient of their father's complete love. She sighed. She would not feel guilt for her father's indiscretions.

Before Boyd Stephenson said goodbye, he had become a friend. He slipped a folded sheet with his contact information in Blossom's hand, "Father might have been pleased to know we've connected," he said.

Blossom was glad when Sheldon came over to where she'd been sitting and said, "Let's take a break … Let's go to our special place." They held hands and walked toward his car.

"Funerals are tough, your father was a very special man, people loved him," Sheldon said, obviously trying to raise Blossom's spirits.

"Rightly so," Blossom said.

She slid into the front passenger seat of Sheldon's car and opened the window.

Their special place was a waterfall that cascaded down the side of a steep hill, forming bubbles in the stream below. Sheldon and Blossom had discovered that place by accident a long time ago when they were exploring the hills. It was their place of refuge.

The sun had already gone down behind the mountain when they got to their special place. The two of them walked hand-in-hand along the narrow path. It was quiet except for the sound of rustling water down the side of the hill.

Blossom remembered all the times they'd sat on the nearby mound and dreamed—bright, sunny days; dusky evenings; and cool, moonlit nights.

She looked up at Sheldon, and his lips met hers. "Bloss, I want you for my wife," he said.

Blossom had hoped Sheldon would allow her more time after the funeral of her father, perhaps weeks, if not months to consider his question. She truly wanted more time to think, to ponder what it would mean if she gave up what she already had in Toronto and returned to Montego Bay. She remained silent. Sheldon kissed her again and again.

"Don't make me wait any longer," Sheldon said.

Blossom knew she had already spent too many years wavering; she was matter-of-fact in her response, "Sheldon, would you marry someone else?"

"I am saying that it's you I want to marry, Bloss; you need not return to Toronto. You know that I love you; I know that you love me. Why the delay? Why, Bloss?"

As much as she loved Sheldon very much, Blossom was determined; she wanted to weigh her decision and then chart her path, her own way.

Later, when the two of them walked to Sheldon's car, he said; "You held up well at your father's funeral, Bloss"

"Thank you Sheldon, you were terrific with keeping the crowd orderly."

"...And Odette worked hard to hold things together for a successful finish." Sheldon added.

"Indeed ... Father would have been proud."

Sheldon pulled into Odette's driveway.

"Stay a while." Blossom whispered. She'd been shedding mournful tears all day.

"I'll stay my love."

Altogether, Blossom remained in Montego Bay for ten days.

On the day of her departure, Blossom woke up at first light. Sheldon had already telephoned and left a message for her: *"Good morning, Bloss ... I love you. Call me when you get to Toronto—goodbye my love."*

With her father's funeral behind her, Blossom was thankful to leave the remaining drama for her mother and her sister Odette to handle.

She was glad to return to her familiar routine in Toronto.

FOURTEEN

Blossom arrived at the office at eight o'clock that morning. Laura's Coffee Bar was already buzzing. Regulars were at the counter eating Laura's delicious homemade muffins and sipping hot drinks. Simpson, the security guard spotted Blossom. "Here's your coffee, Miss Black ... No need to join the long line," he said.

"Thank you, Simpson." Blossom took a deep sip and walked briskly toward the elevators. Her office door on the 14th floor was ajar. Ruby was arranging her desktop. Blossom caught sight of a bouquet of flowers on her credenza.

She read the note: *Nine years with the firm is significant ... let's celebrate by going directly to the Royal York for dinner tonight, Ron.*

Ron knocked and entered Blossom's office "Good morning Blossom … welcome back" he was smiling broadly.

"I'm glad to be back, Ron … How have you been? Thanks for the flowers, they're beautiful!"

"Nine years with the firm … eh? … Impressive!" Ron said.

"Seems like a mighty long time," Blossom smiled softly.

"So dinner is on?" Ron asked.

"Absolutely."

"Then I'll pick you up at seven o'clock tonight and you can tell me about Montego Bay," he smiled.

Dottie Johnson, Seymour Johnson's wife had passed on and Seymour was suffering from chronic arthritis in his joints but that did not faze him. His personal involvement within the firm never diminished and he continued with active law practice.

"I'm glad you agreed to assist me when I go on business trips." Seymour had said to Blossom when he requested her assistance in that regard. She had assured Seymour that it would be a pleasure to assist him.

Lyle Maxwell, a major client, had made several attempts to get Seymour to make the trip to Bermuda to complete a number of trademark deals.

"The deals have to be done down here, I will

cover all expenses," Lyle Maxwell offered during a conference call with Seymour, Ron and Blossom.

"Lyle, old pal ... I'm not allowed to be up in a plane for more than an hour ... Doctor's orders," Seymour had replied.

"What about that bright young lawyer you've got up there, Seymour?" Lyle went on.

"My son, Ron? He's right here. If you like, I'll send him down there to close the deals."

"Send Ron down ... but I'll miss having some good old-time fun with you, Seymour ... We must complete these deals before the end of the month in order to comply with protocols."

"You got it, pal." The men chatted some more before they said goodbye.

Seymour Johnson turned to Blossom and said; "Miss Black, I have faith in your competency and so I'm asking you to work alongside Ron on this assignment."

Not wanting to be disrespectful, Blossom said; "If you are requesting that I accompany Ron ... sir, I've just returned from a business trip in Ottawa and, I had planned to take time off from work in lieu of the days I'd been away."

"It'll only be a three-day trip Miss Black, and anyway, you'll be going south this time ... You could almost call it a mini vacation." Blossom made a funny face and relented. Ron nodded in agreement.

Arrangements were made for Blossom to accompany Ron to Bermuda. They stayed at an old-fashioned inn along the slope of the rolling hillside.

While Ron was completing Lyle Maxwell's trademark and patent deals, Blossom toured the English-centric shops for bargains. She purchased a bale of Irish linen and numerous British souvenirs. Mostly, she attended to Ron's paperwork when he returned to the inn from his daylong meetings.

Ron had been in his suite, reading a book after he'd tied up loose ends in the Maxwell files and Blossom was in her suite preparing luggage for her return flight to Toronto. She heard a light tap on her door, and believing it to be staff ready to take the luggage away, she opened the door that separated the rooms to retrieve Ron's luggage.

She attempted to pulled back remembering she'd been wearing pajama bottoms and a tank top, her hair was in a messy ponytail and she was barefoot.

Ron looked at Blossom with pretend surprise that she'd entered his room without knocking first.

"May I ..." Then she immediately switched her question to an apology. "I'm sorry, Ron ... I didn't realize you were in your room."

Ron smiled.

"Yes, I can help you, Miss Black." He gently placed D.H. Lawrence's Novel; *Lady Chatterley's Lover,* on the table beside him and walked to where Blossom stood. He kissed her squarely on her mouth. "I'm sorry, Miss Black; I couldn't help myself."

Blossom wanted to be kissed—by whom, she was not certain. She returned Ron's kiss, and then she pretended to fall across her bed. He playfully tumbled on top of her. "I have such a great need for you, Blossom" Ron said in a raspy tone.

"And I do too," Blossom replied softly.

"Sweetheart, let me love you now, and we'll go for dinner in the dining room afterwards."

Ron's deep need for Blossom excited her and she responded fittingly to his desire.

"You satisfy my yearning for you ... every time," Ron confessed.

Later in the dining room, over a light meal of salmon and baked potatoes with a variety of local fruits and vegetables, Ron looked at Blossom soberly and said. "Blossom ... I am tired of sneaking around with you ... It's time we bring our relationship out in the open."

Blossom was playful.

Ron touched the tip of her nose; her light freckles were visible, her raw beauty noticeable. He kissed her. "I want *you* only, let's get married."

Blossom was wide-eyed, shocked.

"Get married here?"

"Yes... we do it here ... and we go back to Toronto as Mr. and Mrs. Johnson."

"Give me time, Ron."

You already had time, Blossom."

"Not like that Ron ..." Blossom trailed off.

"You know I love you ... Are you going to keep running away from me?"

"Where would I go?" She teased.

"Let's do it then" Ron said.

Blossom wrapped her arms around Ron's neck and kissed him. She was not yet ready to say yes to Ron. Two men wanted her complete love. The one she truly loved was waiting in Montego Bay for her to say yes to him; the other she could love was looking deep into her eyes and asking her to marry him.

Their plane landed late at Pearson and by the time they cleared customs, it was close to midnight.

"I'll go to the office first to prepare for my meeting with Dad tomorrow morning," Ron said to Blossom as they walked out to passenger pick-up.

It had been a long day, Blossom was anxious to get home. She hailed a cab.

When she arrived at her suite, the phone had been ringing. She quickly opened her front door and kicked off one shoe, the other shoe stayed stuck to her foot. She hopped on the shoeless foot to get to her ringing telephone.

She checked the caller id and recognized her cousin Darlene.

"Hello, Darlene."

"Hello, Bloss."

"How are you?"

"Not as good as you."

Blossom detected a note of cynicism. She had not spoken to Darlene in a long time. She pulled out a chair from under the kitchen table and sat.

"What's up, Darlene?" Blossom was curious.

"I'm calling to tell you about Hansel."

"You're calling to tell me about Hansel?" Blossom repeated.

"Yes. He and Mavis were in a car accident along Queen Elizabeth Way this morning, Blossom. They were coming into Toronto from Hamilton."

"How bad was the accident?"

"Mavis has a broken femur, a broken wrist and some cracked ribs, she will survive. Hansel didn't make it ..."

Blossom gasped. "Dear God ... Darlene ... Are you saying Hansel expired?"

"Yes ... on the way to Etobicoke General Hospital."

"I'm sorry to hear of such a tragedy." Tears immediately flooded Blossom's eyes.

"Poor Hansel," Darlene said, "he never realized his dream of becoming a famous blues singer ... If you wish, I'll keep you posted about the funeral arrangements."

"I'll be obliged if you do, Darlene."

Blossom reflected on Darlene's past disloyalty to her; the time when Darlene colluded with Hansel and tricked her into a sham marriage had lingered in her memory for many years but suddenly it all disappeared.

Hansel's tragic end erased every trace of ill-will Blossom had harbored.

Blossom's eyes caught a large brown envelope from her mother that had been on the kitchen table for a few days, she carefully opened the envelope and newspaper clippings fell to the floor. She read the bold titles.

Local Librarian: Maureen Maria Grant, Weds Businessman Sheldon Jason Morgan.

She was stunned.

FIFTEEN

"I will not be reasonable," Blossom said aloud. Picking up the phone on her desk, she dialed her sister Odette.

"Odie ... I don't believe it."

"You don't believe what, Bloss?"

"Mom sent me news that Sheldon and Maureen are married."

"Mom promised me she'd wait," Odette said.

"Wait? Why wait?" Blossom was on the verge of shouting at her sister.

"Because you'd understand the situation better when Sheldon told you about it himself ... Wish them both well, Bloss."

"Wish them well? How can you say that, Odie? I'm furious." She hung up without saying goodbye.

Blossom knocked and entered Ron office, she had a long face. "Hello Blossom, I can see you're already having a rough day," Ron said and got up from his chair to greet her.

"I'm sorry Ron, I would've waited to inform you about this at our weekly meeting ... but the matter has become quite urgent, I've been called to Montego Bay, as soon as possible ... I'm requesting a week's leave of absence."

"Let's go together this time."

"We were in Bermuda only just weeks ago, remember?" Blossom moaned.

"That was business ... Let's make it a vacation sweetheart. Let's tie the knot down there." Ron was serious.

"This is more family matters that I'm required to attend to, not a vacation."

"Then go safely, and come back quickly," Ron blew Blossom a kiss.

Blossom went back into her office and sulked, nothing made sense. She opened *Fancy Blooms'* trademark file and leafed through several pages, but it was difficult to concentrate on work. She never thought the relationship between Sheldon and Maureen Grant would lead to marriage. She had heard gossip about the two of them and she had dismissed the stories as untrue.

Blossom stared blankly at her unfinished coffee and bran muffin then she set them aside and slid deeper into her chair, the news about Sheldon and

Maureen weighed heavily on her mind. She wanted to be reasonable although she had to take some blame for Sheldon's actions.

He had asked her to marry him more than once, and she had asked him for time to consider. How long did she expect him to wait? She must be pragmatic—it was what it was.

Blossom was in a dark mood, jealousy had consumed her mind. If she wanted to shine a light on her darkened thoughts then Montego Bay was the place to go. With no more unfettered access to Sheldon she felt an instant longing for him. "I will not be defeated—I'll even the score." Blossom said aloud.

She walked over to the coffee machine, poured a fresh cup, and took a long sip. In a few days, she would be in Montego Bay—again.

It had been a long tiring day. Blossom dialed her sister from the telephone on her desk.

"Hello Odie, how are you?

"So-so … I'm queasy every day."

"You'll begin to feel better as the baby continues to grow." Blossom paused. "Can you pick me up at the airport next Thursday Odie?"

"Certainly, I'm glad we've made up."

"We never had a quarrel … I'm looking forward to spending a week with you and Mom. Love you, Odie … Bye." Odette smiled, "Ta-ta Bloss".

Blossom landed in Montego Bay on a warm day in August. She had reflected on her reason for making the trip while she was inflight. She may well see Sheldon during her time in Montego Bay, although she questioned her real motive. She supposed her reason to be home was to clear the gloom she had been feeling.

Montego Bay was in carnival mode.

Blossom spotted Odette's car inching forward in a long line of road traffic. She waited for the car to stop in front of where she stood at the pick-up area. Odette's baby bump was resting on the steering wheel.

"This one is feisty," Odette said, touching her belly. Blossom patted Odette's belly.

"Feisty and large," Blossom observed.

"I have to stop for mangoes," Odette said and navigated over to the roadside to make the purchase from a street vendor.

"I can't wait ... have to eat these mangoes before I drive farther." Odette sank her teeth into the fruit. Blossom watched her sister ate and she wished that someday she would have a similar experience. The two of them chatted and laughed as Odette weaved her way through the stream of traffic. The sisters arrived at their mother's home well before dark. Margareta Black was standing at the gate waiting for her daughters to arrive. Blossom noticed that her mother kept the yard beautiful; her favorite poinsettia tree was green and lush.

"Mom, you look well," Blossom ran into her mother's open arms. Margareta Black hugged and kissed her daughter.

"Come ... dinner is waiting," Margareta said and guided Blossom into the dining room. Blossom's favorite meal of escoveitch snapper fish and white rice was on the dining table.

After dinner, Odette grabbed her sister's hand and pulled her.

"Let's go for a stroll along the beach, Bloss."

"Yes ... let's go."

The late evening breeze was cool, the full moon was reflecting on the ocean, and the sisters were chatting as they walked in paced steps.

"Sheldon is on your mind I can tell," Odette said.

"It's more than that, Odie ... I'm thinking about the mistakes I made by allowing Sheldon to slip away from me ... and it's all because of my indecisiveness."

"Sheldon loves you very much, I know it. Why, you two have been going since you were in college. He's your first love. Sheldon has now moved on Bloss and it looks like you've been moving on. What of your relationship with Mr. Johnson, you've known him for a while, make a decision ..."

Odette became quiet, realizing she had been the only one talking. The silence was long, except for the sound of heavy waves that lashed against the seashore.

"I will not bother Sheldon anymore if he tells me he no longer loves me."

"Sheldon would never tell you he no longer loves you, Bloss, you know it."

The sisters walked hand in hand and talked some more before they headed home. Blossom retired to her room. She had difficulty falling asleep. She got up and went into the kitchen to make cocoa and found her mother sitting at the kitchen table having a nightcap.

"Mom, may I join you?" she asked her mother and pulled out a chair, but instead of sitting in the chair, Blossom sat on her mother's lap and put her arms around her neck. She felt like a little girl again, only, now her father was not with her.

"What brings you back home so soon after your Daddy's burial?" Margareta inquired of her daughter.

"I miss Daddy, Mom ... Being here makes me feel like Daddy is still alive."

"Since he's been gone ... I'm lonely for your Daddy but I have his things around me to remind me of him."

"You and Daddy were in love to the end, Mom ... I love both of you."

"I adored him, honey ... I know your Daddy loved me very much ... I would have carried you whether he married me or not." Margareta wiped a tear. "Your Daddy wouldn't want me to fret over his death. He would want me to be happy."

"... And Alma's Dance School. How is that going, Mom?"

"As you know, I'm now running the school ...

Having the school up and running is a great gift from your father. He purchased exclusive rights and acquired the school after Alma passed; now I own and run the school."

"And, how's Mrs. Grant doing since the stroke?"

"Dorothy no longer engages in lucid conversations. It's been difficult to handle the loss of her friendship."

"It's strange the way Mrs. Grant's health declined rapidly after the death of her husband."

"The stroke just floored Dorothy. After that, dementia crept in, now it looks like Alzheimer's disease"

"I'm sorry, Mom."

Blossom and her mother talked and laughed, and later, before they said goodnight, Blossom buried her head into her mother's shoulder and cried; her mother did not interrupt her crying.

The next morning, Blossom woke up with a nagging urge to telephone Sheldon. She felt a need to have a conversation with him, although she knew she should just congratulate Sheldon and accept that he had become husband to Maureen Grant. Her heart was full of questions—not that Sheldon was obliged to answer any of them, but it would make her feel a lot better if he did.

The morning was already too warm, a sign that it was going to be a hot day. Blossom sat on her mother's back porch wearing tank top and cropped shorts, watching fishermen's boats out at sea and beachcombers trolling along the beach looking for rare finds. Her mother's dog, Sari, started to bark. Blossom looked in the direction of Sari's bark and noticed a silver Mercedes–Benz turning the corner and approaching the long driveway.

It was difficult to discern the lone occupant who was wearing large sunglasses. She watched the car as it made its way slowly up the driveway and stopped at her gate. A horn sounded.

Blossom's mother went out to investigate.

"How is Dorothy doing these days?" Blossom heard her mother asking.

That must be Maureen Grant, Blossom thought as she listened closely to the conversation.

"She has good days, Mrs. Black. Thank you."

"Bloss … guess who's here to visit?" her mother called out.

"Who Mom?" Blossom asked pretending not to recognize Maureen's voice.

"Miss Maureen is visiting us."

Blossom hoped her attire was not too revealing for Miss hoity-toity Maureen Grant. The sound of Maureen's footsteps made Blossom turn around.

"Blossom … how … are … you?" Maureen asked, stopping just short of knocking over a chair as she came around the bend. Blossom was unprepared to respond to the sarcasm she detected in Maureen's voice. She thought for a moment and then replied.

"I am fine," with enough disdain to alert Maureen she would not be accommodating her surprise visit. Blossom considered offering Maureen a seat, but first, she wanted to know the reason for Maureen's social call.

Blossom's mother appeared with two tall tumblers of iced tea. Margareta Black had always relished the idea that someday she would talk about Sheldon as her son.

"He's a nice boy ... has manners," Margareta had said when Blossom introduced Sheldon, and although Margareta was disappointed that Blossom had let Sheldon slipped away from her, she never meddled in her daughter's affairs.

Margareta pulled out a chair for Maureen and handed her a tumbler with ice tea.

"Please sit, Miss Maureen," she said.

Maureen set her tumbler on the patio table and sat with her legs crossed.

"My dear Bloss, it's good to see you," she began, "I'm sorry that I never got an opportunity to offer my sympathies at your father's funeral, and when I came to visit, you had already left for Toronto."

"A phone call would've been nice."

"Yes, of course ... and I also wanted to tell you that Sheldon and I were dating ... you and I being friends and all ..." Maureen's voice trailed off.

"We've connected regularly in the past Maureen, there were plenty of chances to tell me."

"That is true," Maureen said, looking chic in her white linen Capri pants and white organza shirt pulled loosely over a white strapless top. She displayed well-manicured finger and toenails done in red polish. Her long braided hair hung loosely along the center of her back and held in place with her sunglasses.

"Blossom," Maureen paused, "I'm not here to apologize for marrying Sheldon ... I'm well aware of your history with him, I am here to renew our friendship and to ask that there be no hard feelings between us because of him. But I must caution you, don't be coming to Montego Bay when it pleases you to rekindle your relationship with Sheldon." Blossom was infuriated. How dare Maureen Grant come into her home and speak to her in that manner?

"In other words, Maureen, you're here to tell me, you stole my boyfriend, you're married to him now, and you would like me and you to still be friends. No damn way." Blossom's was livid.

Maureen shot back in response.

"Touché, Blossom, Sheldon ceased to be your boyfriend a long time ago. I married Sheldon because he was available ... I know the life you lead ... Is your secret lover in Toronto not enough for you?"

Blossom felt uneasy; she sensed a skirmish brewing and she began to tremble. She summoned up some saliva to moisten her dry lips.

"What—the cat got your tongue, Blossom Black? I asked you, is your secret lover in Toronto not enough for you? The man you believe no one else knows about?"

Blossom slowly and deliberately rested her tumbler on the table beside her chair; her temper had risen above fever pitch, and she was losing control of her senses. She shot a nasty look at Maureen.

"Maureen Grant ..." Blossom said her voice a mere whisper. "Shut your mouth! You know nothing about what I do in Toronto ... and anyway, what I do is none of your blasted business!"

Maureen drew in a deep breath.

"Does it feel good to fuck your boss, also known as your boyfriend, so that you can keep your big cushy job?"

Maureen was thrilled to throw dirt at Blossom by letting her know that gossip about her had been circulating. She had clearly come for a fight. Blossom cast her mind back; she could not remember Maureen ever being so vulgar.

Blossom felt a need to defend herself even if there were some truths to Maureen's assertion. She firmly tucked her lower lip under her upper lip, it might be too late to hold back, for she was about to smack Maureen Grant into oblivion.

"I said ... shut the fuck up, Maureen Grant, before I give you a fat lip." Blossom was on her feet; her breathing had become short and heavy. Her mouth was dry. She was ready to put her words into action when suddenly she remembered the time she hit Maureen over the head with her lunchbox in junior school. The hit had raised a swelling at the back of her head. Blossom had promised herself that she would never display her anger in such a hostile way—ever.

You knew about my relationship with Sheldon from the beginning, and yet you betrayed me. I will not let you have Sheldon. You may be wearing his ring but his heart belongs to me. Screw you! Blossom wanted to say.

Blossom inhaled deeply, she felt uncomfortable about saying what was in her heart. Instead, she fixed her eyes directly on Maureen and said.

"Honestly, Maureen, how can you feel justified in doing this to me? I cannot stand to lose Sheldon because I love him but I have no choice than to accept what is… So let's bring this argument to a close, shall we?" Blossom was conciliatory.

Maureen stood her ground, she insisted on making a point. She looked Blossom in the eyes and replied.

"It's not about you Blossom … It's about *me*. Sheldon made me his wife. You really never deserved him, he's mine now …" Maureen turned and looked out to the beach, she lowered her sunglasses over her eyes as if to hide her tears.

Maureen sighed: *It makes no sense; we were little girls together, went through all the grades in school together, we attended the same church and our mothers were the best of friends, how could our love for one man put an end to our close friendship?*

Maureen snatched up her car keys from the tabletop and stormed off to her car. She made the turn along the driveway leading up to her residence and parked alongside Sheldon's unoccupied SUV. She did not want to confront him at that moment.

* * *

Maureen Grant reflected. Her mother had been concerned upon learning she was dating Sheldon Morgan. "Mo, honey ...You know the chatter that's been going around about Blossom and Sheldon."

"Mom, Blossom has a successful career in Toronto; she'll never come back here to live."

"Perhaps not dear but Blossom's been dating Sheldon Morgan for a long time. And she comes to Montego Bay for regular holidays to see him." Dorothy Grant had been matter-of-fact with her daughter.

"*Dating*. That's all it had been Mom. I think people make too much of Sheldon's relationship with Blossom. Just because they've known each other a long time, it doesn't mean their relationship is serious."

"All the same dear, I'm asking you not to let your relationship with Sheldon cause hatred between you and Blossom."

"I won't Mom, I promise." Maureen had assured her mother.

Nevertheless, Maureen decided she would seriously consider Sheldon for a husband. She had read about women who were audacious enough to pop the marriage question to men whom they loved. Maureen did not hold back. At thirty-seven, Maureen was not young yet not old, but she was concerned that opportunities for marriage were not coming her way. She would have liked to be married or to have a lifelong partner. Who wouldn't? It would be nice to share her thoughts with a soul mate and have his children. Many of the girls whom she had grown up with had started families with the men who worked in local industries.

Maureen thought back to an amusing school day she'd spent with Blossom. They'd been in the library. Blossom was reading the last Chapter of *Moby Dick* for Literature class.

"Bloss, let's go for a soda down at Jerry's shop," Maureen had said.

"Certainly Mo, I'll finish this chapter and then we'll go."

The two girls skipped down to Jerry's shop, giggling at the idea that prissy Miss Telma Brown had been asked to the high school dance by Henry Williams, the nerdy math whiz. Telma and Henry had been sitting on the garden bench outside Jerry's shop eating snow cone and kissing each other without regard for prying eyes.

"Henry is by no means socially impaired," Maureen had said to Blossom as they giggled all the way up to the soda counter.

Maureen had wondered if years later she and Blossom would be the same giddy girlfriends. She, the prim one wearing long skirts, became the town's librarian, and Blossom, the vivacious one wearing the tiniest of miniskirts, enjoying a rewarding career in Toronto.

* * *

Blossom's visit to Montego Bay did not dull the unhappiness she'd been feeling. She summoned Odette to drive her to the airport the next day for an early return to Toronto.

Blossom sat in the airport lounge at Sangster's, waiting on stand-by, still reeling from Maureen's uninvited appearance at her mother's place. Suddenly, she heard Sheldon's voice calling through the open door. Blossom jumped up from her chair and ran to him, forgetting he'd been married to Maureen. He put his arms around her, moving in to kiss her, but then pulled back, remembering he was Maureen's husband and he had some explaining to do.

"Bloss I thought I heard wrong ... I just heard that you had come back. There's something I want to tell you."

You should have told me before you married Maureen, Blossom wanted to say. Instead, she said, "I know what you want to tell me, Sheldon ... Your wife Maureen already told me."

"I'm sorry Bloss, please give me a chance to explain ... I'd like to tell you how this came about. Please, let me tell my story."

Blossom felt her world crashing around her. The trip had been a waste of time. She had hoped, that Sheldon would say it was not so, that he had not really married Maureen. That it was all a ruse to get her to come back to him. But instead she saw the regret in his eyes. She made up her mind. She did not want to stay a minute longer.

"I must go, Sheldon, I need to get away so that I can think. I will call you from Toronto." Sheldon thrust his hands in his jeans pockets and slowly walked to his car. Brooding.

Sheldon had always relied on his faith to direct and guide him. He confessed there were two women in his life—a complication he'd never asked for—Blossom Black, the woman who'd captured his heart on a stormy night many years earlier and Maureen Grant, the town's librarian whom he married.

Sheldon had disclosed to his mother that he and wife Maureen were not off to a good start. He'd asked her if she thought he was being punished for not completing seminary.

"Sheldon, dear," his mother had replied in a soft tone, "you're struggling to clear your mind of Blossom Black ... take your time, it will happen. The choice you made to marry Maureen Grant is a good one, Maureen is a good girl. Try and make your marriage work."

"Mother, how can I make something work when I know it won't work?"

"You're right, son ... Did not your father and I try to make you a preacher?" Sheldon was willing to try, if only to please his mother.

* * *

Back in his office, Sheldon was depressed. He had heard that Blossom had been in Montego Bay and he had rushed to Sangster's Airport to see her before she returned to Toronto, mainly to level with her about his decision to marry Maureen. But Blossom would have none of it. His only hope was she would phone him from Toronto as she'd promised.

SIXTEEN

Blossom returned to Toronto with a heavy heart, feeling foolish. She couldn't stifle her desire for Sheldon Morgan, and she regretted the way she and Maureen Grant had parted after the nasty confrontation at her mother's place. There were loose ends that were left dangling. Blossom hated loose ends. She dialed.

"Hello, Sheldon." She hoped he would be excited to hear her voice. He was.

"Hello, Bloss! I thought you'd never speak to me again."

Oh yes, Sheldon, not only will I speak to you, I will see you. You, Sheldon Morgan, will always remember that I am the one you love. The words were not uttered.

"You wanted to talk, Sheldon?"

"Bloss, you already heard."

"You're right, I already heard, but I didn't hear it from you."

"I will explain."

"You will explain? How? Where? When?" Blossom sighed and continued, "Okay … I will give you a chance to explain. Next month I have some more time off. I'll meet with you in Montego Bay."

Sheldon agreed to meet with Blossom. This time, she would give him an opportunity to explain and she would try to be cool, calm and collected.

The thought of Sheldon and Maureen together was *killing* her. Suddenly she felt an urgent need for him. She scurried to her shower and stood under the warm spray with her head tilted upward. The shower turned misty. She imagined Sheldon in the shower with her, lathering her entire body with thick, rich, suds. He was giving his full attention to her inner thighs, his fingers probing. She pictured him inserting, and working with uninterrupted precision. She imagined her total submission, in all the ways she'd intended and how weak she'd felt under his magic charm. When he had fully satisfied her, he laid her pliant body on the bathroom floor, the makeshift altar of their love.

The shower turned cold. Blossom wrapped herself in a warm towel and walked into her garment closet. Hangers with dresses of different colors, makes, designs and lengths were on display. She selected a simple knee-length black dress with plunging neckline and thin shoulder straps, she put on purple sling back shoes and she let her hair down, to the middle of her back. From her favorite spot in her suite, she looked down. The scenery was magnificent. The night was perfect for her dinner with Ron Johnson.

There was a soft knock. Blossom opened the door. Ron stood casually, holding a large brown shopping bag. He looked relaxed in sweats and running shoes.

"Hello, Ron. We're going out for dinner tonight. Yes?"

"Wow! Bloss, you're beautiful in your black dress." Ron had a sneaky smile.

He walked in. "I brought the ingredients. I'm making dinner for you tonight—lasagna."

Blossom kissed Ron on the cheeks. "I cannot let you make me dinner." She said in a serious tone. He pulled her gently into his embrace and kissed her on the lips.

"I make a delicious plate of lasagna, my grandmother's recipe."

The imaginary sexual encounter she had had with Sheldon in the shower minutes earlier was still fresh in her thoughts. She wanted Ron; every part of her confirmed her need. Ron sensed Blossom's desire. He was ready to respond accordingly.

"I can tell that you want me," he said.

"I do Ron ... take me now" Blossom replied.

"Your wish is my command, Ma'am. How much of me do you want?" Ron's voice was huskier than Blossom had ever heard it. The thought of sexually commanding Ron captured Blossom's imagination.

While rotating her shoulders, Blossom said, "Mister Johnson, I demand a full body massage."

In one swoop, Ron picked her up and carried her into the bedroom. He placed her, face down, on her Persian rug and slowly massaged her delicate body from her shoulders down to the tips of her toes. When Ron had completed the task, he quietly moved away and headed toward the kitchen.

"Wait … wait a minute, Johnson," Blossom called out to Ron. "You have more work to do."

Ron swung around.

"There's more?" he asked, with a raised eyebrow.

"Absolutely."

"How may I be of service to you, Ma'am?"

Blossom reached up and pull Ron into the bed. Ron could not hold back. He immediately took possession of Blossom, and the aftermath of their lovemaking was complete satisfaction.

In the stillness that followed, Blossom admitted, if only to herself, that each time she'd made love with Ron she'd satisfied her desire to be with Sheldon Morgan. She looked sideways at the romantic man lying next to her, sound asleep and glistening with perspiration. Soon, she would be disloyal to him one more time—she had to go to Sheldon.

SEVENTEEN

Odette answered the phone after two rings.

"I'll be home next Tuesday, Odie."

"So soon?" Odette asked. It had been just over a month since Blossom's last visit.

"I'm going crazy, Odie ... I must see Sheldon ... My heart is hurting." Odette was silent.

"Sheldon will pick me up at the airport."

"Sheldon will pick you up? Why?"

"Because ..."

Odette waited.

"Why am I not picking you up, Bloss?"

"Because your baby bump will be too big to fit behind the steering wheel."

Odette knew her sister could not be put off.

"But seriously ... when Sheldon picks me up at the airport, we'll head straight to Cool Runnings to eat. We'll have a heart-to-heart conversation; then he'll drop me off at Mom's ... I'm a big girl, Odie I can handle myself. Love you, bye."

"Rise and shine, Miss Black."

Blossom and her assistant, Ruby Snipes, had been in the office until 12:30 in the morning preparing Ron's presentation for an important meeting. Blossom was worried that if she became too comfortable when she got to her apartment, she may not wake up on time to catch her flight to Montego Bay, so she requested concierge to give her a wake-up call. The call came at exactly five o'clock, A.M.

It had been a clear November morning; Blossom was on her way to a warm place. Since there was no need to overdress she wore a white, strapless wool crepe dress with white wedge heel sandals. She pulled a red cardigan over her shoulders, but the cardigan would go into her duffle bag just as soon as she landed in Montego Bay.

In no time, Blossom was in a cab and on her way to Pearson Airport. She was glad to have made it with time left for coffee and toasted bagel from the coffee stand, and a quick glance at the headlines, from a *Globe* newspaper.

Blossom settled into her window seat in first class and pulled the blinds down. She was ready for a quick snooze. She closed her eyes and slept without her thoughts roaming around in her head unchecked.

"You had a good rest?"

She raised her wrist to look at her watch. She had been sleeping for over an hour.

"Yes," she answered the man sitting next to her. She noticed that he was wearing light brown slacks and an exotic shirt—the kind with illustrations of palm trees and bongo drums all over. His black leather attaché case, with the initials DOC, was on the shelf in front of his seat; several sheets of white printed paper were showing.

"My name is David Clark," he said and extended his hand across to Blossom.

"Hello ... Nice to meet you, Mr. Clark ... My name is Blossom Black." She smiled.

David Clark looked at Blossom closely. When she smiled he recalled a similar smile. And those eyes ... those eyes meant something. He'd looked into those eyes before. Then he called to mind—The Emerald Place. He didn't want to disclose his connection to The Emerald Place. He didn't want to be labeled a jerk either. He pretended to be probing.

"I think we've met someplace before. Where have we met?" He asked Blossom, feeling annoyed with himself for not being forthright about where he'd actually met her. She shrugged politely and pretended not to be concerned.

"You've never seen me before? ... Anywhere? ... In the past?" He quizzed, clearly surprised that the lady did not recognize him. Blossom shook her head from side to side. David suddenly became quiet; Blossom thought he might be searching for another pick-up line when she heard him say, "Yes, yes, now I remember. You were coming out of the grocery store at The Emerald Place in Etobicoke early one morning, when you bumped me. It happened a few years ago—five, maybe six years ago."

"And you remember from that long ago?" Blossom asked, trying hard to recollect the incident.

"My office used to be on the third floor in the commercial block at The Emerald Place back then."

Blossom was surprised that David recalled such detail ... How old was he, she thought. Late fifties? Sixtyish? If David remembered all of what he relayed as having happened more than five years earlier and he'd only bumped into her once, then it was likely he knew more than he was telling.

"I'm renting a suite in Tower 2 ... I've lived there, going on six years," Blossom disclosed. David smiled. He was not showing too much excitement over Blossom's revelation that she'd been a tenant in one of The Emerald Place condominium suites all those years. He already knew she was the tenant who occupied the suite on the 21st floor that was intended for him and his family.

It was true, many times he'd considered saying hello to her when he'd seen her entering Building 2, but as the owner of the complex, he would not be presumptuous with his tenants. He adjusted his seat and closed his eyes.

Fate had given David Clark an opportunity to have a conversation with the woman he'd secretly admired. He heard her soft breathing; he opened his eyes and looked at her, and she was asleep. If he were clever, he would make this connection worthwhile, but he had to admit he did not quite remember the basics of socializing at the level he had in mind. Blossom opened her eyes and looked sideways at David. He smiled at her and continued the conversation from where he'd left off.

"I am traveling to Montego Bay to attend a meeting of contractors. My granite company in Ocho Rios submitted an application to provide the marble and granite required for construction on a new hotel and convention center in Portsmore. It's an enormous project requiring a large amount of marble and granite, I hope I win the contract." David smiled. "So, why are you going to Montego Bay?"

"Vacation," Blossom answered, trying not to show too much interest in the curious businessman sitting next to her. She was surprised that David spoke so freely about his business and himself.

Blossom pulled out a magazine from the pocket in front of her seat. She turned the pages slowly. Her thoughts flashed back to the previous night in a conversation with her sister. She confessed she'd been far too casual during their exchange about her *sudden* change of plans upon her arrival in Montego Bay. She recalled that Odette was none too happy when she learned the details.

"Odie ... Sheldon and I will be spending a week together at a private place and then I'll spend the rest of my vacation with you and Mom."

"You and Sheldon will be doing what!!"

"Sheldon and I will be spending ..."

"I heard you, Bloss," Odette butted in. "I am worried about the two of you. You don't have to tell me where you plan to stay ... just phone me now and then while you're hiding out. Montego Bay is not as big a place as you think. You may run into someone who knows you both ..." she trailed off.

Blossom fully understood the implications of being with Sheldon but she refused to dwell on it.

"Odie, I'm a grown woman, you and Mom shouldn't worry about me so much. I'll be fine." She assured her sister.

"Ladies and gentlemen, this is your captain speaking ..."

Blossom opened her eyes, adjusted her seat to the upright position and fastened her seatbelt for landing. The view over Montego Bay was breathtaking.

When the plane came to a full stop, she reached up to retrieve her carry-on bag from the overhead rack. David Clark said, "Let me."

Both of them exited the plane together and moved through customs in record time. They stepped out into a sudden gust of cool breeze at passenger pick up. Blossom's white strapless wool crepe dress swirled around her, and her hair gave way to the breeze. There was a car waiting for David.

"Mr. Clark, welcome. I'll take your luggage, sir," the driver said.

David Clark touched Blossom's elbow. "May I offer you a ride?" he asked her.

"Thank you Mr. Clark. I have a ride," she answered politely.

"Give me a call when you get back to Toronto," David said, handing a gold printed business card to Blossom. "Give me a call," he repeated as if to make sure she'd heard him.

Just then, Blossom saw Sheldon's lean figure coming toward her. He was carefully hooking his sunglasses on his shirt pocket.

Blossom walked into Sheldon's open arms.

EIGHTEEN

At last, the day had arrived; Blossom would spend a week with Sheldon at a private place, and if all went according to her plans, she would discover in a month or so that she was carrying his child. She felt a tad worried; maybe she should call off her willful plan before she even began, although having Sheldon Morgan's child was exactly what Blossom planned when she learned that Sheldon had married Maureen Grant her childhood friend and archrival—too late now, she would not accommodate cold feet.

She recognized that the consequences of her plan would ruin other lives and cause untold heartaches, but the only thing on her mind was an outward manifestation of her love for Sheldon. She was determined to possess a part of Sheldon Morgan—his child to complete their love; she would never again be lonely. She sighed. What of Ron Johnson? This was no time to second-guess or search for answers, she justified.

Sheldon closed his big hands around Blossom's waist. He picked her up, looked deep into her bluish-green eyes and said. "Gosh! You have no idea how much I've been looking forward to seeing you, Bloss," then he put her down softly.

"When was the last time you had a bite to eat?" Sheldon asked Blossom, lifting her luggage and carefully placing it into the trunk of his SUV.

"This morning ... toasted bagel and coffee in the airport lounge in Toronto."

"Let's have some lunch then." Sheldon helped Blossom into the passenger seat and they drove off.

They found their way to their favorite table at Cool Runnings and had a meal of chicken salad papaya juice and fresh fruits, Blossom remarked, "That was delicious."

"Let's stay awhile," Sheldon said and then signaled the waiter to come.

"May I order you a drink, Bloss? Tonic water ... Rum and coke?"

"I'll have tonic water please."

"Tonic water for the lady, rum and coke for me," Sheldon said to the waiter.

Sheldon turned a soft look at Blossom. "Want to listen to music?" Blossom nodded. Sheldon walked over to the jukebox and selected some familiar songs.

"Shall we sit on the sofa over there?" Sheldon pointed to a deep-cushioned sofa in a private area. Blossom relaxed her head against his shoulder. With the two of them, there were no pretenses. He wanted her and his loin began to show.

"You want me ... don't you Bloss?

"I do," Blossom whispered. She'd been trying hard to forget the truth about who Sheldon had become—he *was* Maureen Grant's husband and it was too late to change that now.

The lights at Cool Runnings started to click on, and Sheldon looked at Blossom. "Night is coming, Bloss ... Shall we go?"

Sheldon put down a generous tip and escorted Blossom to his SUV.

They travelled through a picturesque rural community to their destination.

With the windows down, the night breeze had its way with Blossom's hair as Sheldon drove at a moderate speed.

"Sheldon, the scenery is magnificent."

"Without question, my love. The view is much more pleasing during daylight hours ... The return trip will be even more appealing." Sheldon was pleased to have Blossom seated beside him.

They arrived at Moonbeams-On-The-Hill, a small inn nestled in banana greenery on a hill overlooking the sea. Sheldon drove up to the wrought iron gate and gained permission to proceed along the driveway that led to the front door.

A long time ago, Moonbeams-On-The-Hill used to be a plantation home belonging to a rich banana grower named James Hill. The home changed hands several times and eventually was refurbished for resort accommodation.

Blossom and Sheldon entered the foyer. It was furnished with elongated side tables and Victorian-style high-back chairs. The large chandelier in the center of the ceiling was luminous, and the drapery and wall hangings were floral, olive green and chocolate brown. Dwarf palm trees were well positioned in corners—it was a most inviting place to spend their week.

"Welcome," the clerk at the front desk smiled.

"Come with me, ma'am, and sir," the bellhop said, lifting their luggage and guiding them along a short passage that opened into a cozy sitting area with similar but fewer furnishings than those in the lobby.

Adjacent to the sitting area was a double door that opened to a beautifully decorated bedroom. The olive green drapes were pulled to each side of the wall-to-wall window. Everything was lovely. Floral cushions of different sizes decorated the full size chaise lounge.

Soft moonlight shone through the venetian blinds casting horizontal lines on the opposite wall. Blossom noticed a large urn with anthuriums on a table beside the queen-sized bed.

Sheldon watched as Blossom admired the anthuriums and read the accompanying note that ended, "Love you, Sheldon." He gently turned Blossom around to face him and kissed her, long and hard. He felt pressure building up in him. He had not felt so much tension in a long time.

"I've wanted to kiss you like this from the moment I laid my eyes on you at the airport this afternoon," Sheldon lifted Blossom onto the bed. Her white wool crepe dress gave way as he slowly unzipped the back, showing her strapless bra.

"Let's take this thing off." He was impatient, yet sensitive. He slowly unfastened the back of her bra, and her breasts tumbled into his big hands. He could not hold back; he took her breasts as they surrendered to his lips. When he raised his head, he heard Blossom saying, "Mr. Morgan ... Don't forget ... you are now a married man."

Blossom was thirty-seven years old; Sheldon was forty-one. It was not his first time with her, and she wasn't going to pretend she was shy; both of them had been yearning for this moment. She was prepared to give Sheldon all of the love she'd stored up for him, and for his part, he was ready to take all of the love she would give him.

"I want you, Bloss ...You belong to me ... every part of you is mine to have."

"I'm yours, take me Sheldon."

In the blink of an eye, Sheldon sent his clothes flying. There was no time for appropriateness.

He'd been longing for Blossom for many months and now that she was in his arms he felt like he was about to explode. He guided his magnificently expanded shoot deep down to the bottom of her mossy-covered core and she clasped him. The two of them joined and their bodies stilled for a fleeting moment before Sheldon began to work.

"Holy Jesus, please forgive me." Sheldon whimpered as he worked with care and accuracy, sweat beads popping out all over his forehead.

"Sheldon, you satisfy me" Blossom whimpered, she was burning up with desire.

She wanted to conceive Sheldon's baby; she hoped this would be the moment that he poured his love into her and gave her the child she longed for.

All through the night, they claimed each other as though they rightfully belonged.

The next morning, they were silent over breakfast of coffee, orange juice, boiled eggs, toast, and fresh fruits. Sheldon finally broke the silence.

"I cannot forgive myself for the way in which our relationship is ending, I made you a promise, I told you I'd wait for you and I broke my promise."

"Shhhhhh…" Blossom said and gently placed an index finger on his lips to silence him. "Yesterday is gone; this moment is what we have."

"It's not that simple, Bloss," Sheldon said with a sigh. "I hurt your feelings … I'm sorry."

Blossom shook her head from side to side. "My heart is still intact," she whispered. "… My feelings would've been hurt had I not spend this time with you, I love you Sheldon." She smiled softly.

The following afternoon, Sheldon had been on the tennis court with his newfound tennis partner while Blossom sat leisurely by the pool sipping rum and coke. She was aware that her ovules were exploding—ready to connect. She was itching to have Sheldon inside of her. As if reading her mind, Sheldon suddenly appeared. He was breathless and dripping with perspiration. "What's wrong Sheldon" Blossom queried.

"Honey ... I lost all four sets, Jerome beat the crap out of me ... Anyway, all I could think about while I was on the tennis court was making love to you." He smiled and slowly released the floral tie from Blossom's hair. He tilted her sunglasses atop her head and kissed her deeply, and her body automatically went into acceptance mode. He gently pulled her up with both hands so that her full length lined up against him. He groaned, signifying his loin was expanding. "Let's go to our room."

The mating call was loud; Sheldon was calling and Blossom was already answering. She rushed ahead along the passageway, past the sitting area, and into their suite. She barely made it to the chaise. Sheldon was in pursuit. He could not have made it any farther than the chaise lounge.

Blossom presented herself to Sheldon with no reservations, and he took her without regrets. They laid-back on the soft cushions that lined the chase, not moving, not speaking, feeling as one with each other and loving the silent communion.

That evening, Blossom and Sheldon ate dinner in the main dining room. She wore a short, black, strapless dress. Her hair cascaded down the center of her back, the way Sheldon liked it; her beautifully tapered legs curved slightly in a pair of black six-inch patent shoes and she carried a patent clutch purse under one arm.

"Bloss ... you're gorgeous ... I want everyone to look at you," Sheldon stared at Blossom with open mouth. She pleased him in every way and he wondered *how come* she was not his wife. They sat down to a meal of lobster tails and steamed vegetables, and they each had a glass of white wine.

They'd been dancing in the ballroom to Ben E. King's romantic ballad, "This Magic Moment." Sheldon savored the beauty that rested against his chest. There was so much he loved about her; he'd been a fool to relinquish her. He tilted her head and kissed her. The two of them swayed to the music.

Blossom felt Sheldon's twitch; he had become solid against her. She moved in sync to find a comfortable position as he pressed her into him. His spasms aroused her, and both of them knew it was time to yield to the burning desire that had been building up in their bodies. They dashed off to their suite, in obedience to nature's call.

Blossom laid flat on her back with both knees bent to welcome Sheldon's chiseled size. He was swollen rock-hard, she was moist and pliant, and they soared together, higher and higher, in bliss. Two people who couldn't stop loving each other celebrated their completeness on their terms, and if Blossom got the desire of her heart, she would be the happiest woman in the world.

Sheldon woke up early the next morning while Blossom was sound asleep. He kissed her softly before he put on sweats for a stroll along the silent beach. As he walked, he looked toward the still water as if asking for its help in solving the puzzle of his personal life.

He recalled his mother's advice not to put all of his eggs in one basket, which might not have been the best advice she'd given him. He admitted his decision to transfer some of his eggs to another basket led him to marry Maureen Grant.

He should let Blossom go, he thought as he stared blankly out to the skyline.

He admitted, he had known about her relationship in Toronto and he should have pursued her when he found out, but he was selfish; he could not bring himself to give up his successful business in Montego Bay. He felt a tingle in his eyes. Blossom was a beautiful bird that was not meant to be caged. He had to let her fly.

He kicked the sand under his feet several times then he let out a sigh, cognizant of the unavoidable end to his relationship with her.

Blossom cuddled under the warm duvet. When she flung an arm across the bed to where Sheldon had been laying—he was not there. She looked out the window and saw him walking along the beach.

"Sheldon!" Blossom called out. He beckoned her to join him. The two of them walked hand in hand leaving imprints of their bare feet in the wet sand.

"You make me so happy," Blossom said.

Sheldon smiled.

"Are you ready for breakfast?" he asked, bruising her neck with a deep kiss.

"Yes… Let's have breakfast in bed." Blossom was playful.

"Then race me to our suite, Baby." Sheldon started to sprint, and then he slowed down and allowed Blossom to overtake him.

"I won … I won," Blossom exclaimed and jumped on the bed.

"I let you win," Sheldon teased and playfully threw himself on top of her. Then he impishly pulled at her halter top and it came loose without effort.

Blossom's breasts glistened in the natural light. Sheldon inhaled deeply.

"I love you," he said softly.

He could not suppress his immediate desire. He took her fully, methodically. And when he was sure he'd sufficiently pleased her; both of them enjoyed breakfast in bed.

It appeared to Blossom like time had sped by since they'd arrived at Moonbeams-On-The-Hill. They'd fully relished each other's sweetness, and they were still hungry for more. Blossom reached for Sheldon's hand, "Let's go for a walk along the trails."

"Yes, let's go," he agreed.

Blossom's long cotton dress lightly brushed her thighs as she walked along the trails and the warm summer breeze ruffled her hair, to Sheldon's delight. The two of them gathered wild flowers, and chased elusive butterflies until they were exhausted. Then they came to rest at a shaded area. Sheldon laid his head in Blossom's lap and closed his eyes.

"Happy?" Blossom asked him.

"Being here with you like this? Yes, my love ... I'm extremely happy. Let's extend our stay one more day," Sheldon begged. "Let's not," Blossom moaned.

Sheldon reached up and carefully undid the tiny buttons at the front of her shirt. He paused at the sight of her breasts and buried his head in the hollow between them; he took her breasts, right then and there. His loin stiffened and he knew he had to have her. They made love under the shade and reached the top of their passion together. Nothing she'd experienced in the past had prepared her for the overwhelming ecstasy that consumed her.

Sheldon had been loading their luggage in the trunk of his SUV, for their return journey, "Oh, my goodness ... I must phone Odie, the cops will be out looking for us as missing persons," Blossom laughed. "Whatever will be, will be," Sheldon chuckled.

"Not a chance, Sheldon Morgan ... I'll phone my

sister this minute." Blossom laughed quietly. She phoned Odette from the Lobby of Moonbeams-On-The-Hill.

As expected, Odette scolded Blossom.

"The next time you choose to go MIA, do not inform me ahead of time. Mom and I will wait up for you, be safe." Odette said. The sisters laughed and then said ta-ta.

Sheldon navigated the winding countryside with practiced skill, assured by the soft buzz of his SUV.

"Look! Sheldon the road sign says 10 miles to Warwick Junction."

"Ten miles too soon, my love." Sheldon looked sideways at Blossom and smiled. He knew Warwick Junction was the point at which he'd make the final turn to Blossom's mother's home.

The road curved without warning, showing a vast expanse of sugarcane fields and orange groves, crisscrossed in neatly laid rows. She noticed how the valley below circled the hill on one side like a broad green belt. Farther away, cattle grazed lazily in the grassy meadow.

Blossom lowered the passenger side window for a better view. Banana leaves swayed in the late afternoon wind and the magnificent Blue Mountain Peak reached toward the sky, evidence of the absolute beauty of nature. A farmer sat on the side of the road eating his lunch as his mother cow, heavy with calf, slowly sauntered across the road, forcing Sheldon to stop. Blossom gasped as a passenger bus made a wide turn around the opposite corner to avoid a cyclist.

"Sheldon ... let's rest for a while."

"Good idea," he smiled.

Both of them walked hand in hand along the dirt path that led downhill. The blue skies, the greenery and the quiet stream were welcoming. The day was perfect. Blossom touched the stream with her toes. The only audible sound was the slow trickle of water down the stream.

Out of the blue, Maureen Grant came into Blossom's thoughts.

"Sheldon how's Maureen?" the words spilled without effort. Sheldon stopped abruptly. His eyes followed the flow of the stream. He reflected, likely searching for the right answer. He had attempted to explain his side of the story when they were at Moonbeams-On-The-Hill and, although he never accepted it until that very moment, he admitted, the subject made him nervous. He knew the moment would come and yet he never wanted to deal with it. He hadn't felt as uncomfortable in a long time. He drew in a tense breath, well aware that Blossom was waiting for an answer. He sighed. All he wanted was to have the memories of his time with her fresh and imprinted for all time on his mind.

Sheldon placed a finger under Blossom's chin and tilted her face up.

"I love you, Bloss, I've loved you a long time," he paused, "Maureen and I developed a relationship, I admit, I married her when she became pregnant with my child, which was the right thing to do."

"Maureen is expecting your baby!"

"She miscarried at three months."

"I'm sorry."

"Don't be sorry; it was all my fault. I neglected Maureen. I spent too much time away from her. I know Maureen loves me, I would return her love but *my* love for you is very strong. My heart will not release me to any other woman."

Blossom gazed intently at Sheldon. She studied his expression. She saw a look of sincerity in his eyes.

"I was foolish, I should've said yes to your love." Sheldon looked toward the stream and shook his head from side to side, "It is so unfair," he said.

"What *is so unfair*, Sheldon?" Blossom asked.

"It is unfair that I waited all these years ... and for what? To marry Maureen Grant instead of you."

"I had asked you to wait for me, even as I kept up an affair in Toronto. I'm equally responsible for the way things turned out," Blossom confessed. "Please forgive me, Sheldon." **she begged**.

Sheldon deliberated. "Ron Johnson is his name? I've known about him. Bloss, I knew you veered off on a different path, I should've come after you but I didn't, I gave you space ... I waited for you to say yes to *me*, I truly wanted you for my wife." Sheldon drew in a deep breath. "I got tired of waiting."

Blossom let out an audible sigh.

"Are you alright, Bloss?" Sheldon asked her.

"I've lost your love ... I know it." she answered.

* * *

The front porch lights clicked on when Blossom reached her mother's home. Odette ran toward her sister with open arms, "Come, give your demanding sister a big hug."

Margareta Black watched her two daughters as they hugged and kissed. She'd always admired how easy it had been for them to express their love for each other.

Blossom noticed Sheldon putting her luggage by the front door. She held out her hands toward him, he took her hands and pressed them over his heart. Both of them stood silent for a long moment. Sheldon spoke first.

"The past few days never happened ...Let's just kiss and say goodbye ..."

He kissed her nose and then he turned to leave. Blossom pulled on his shirt.

Sheldon, you may want me to believe this past week never happened, but I know it did. It happened the way I intended. It happened the way I wanted it to remain in my memory and if, for some reason, the result is not the way I expected, I will remember it was my desire to have your child ... to bind me to you ... forever. The words were soundless.

Blossom closed her eyes; she felt the tingle of tears and she blinked to release a trickle as it rolled down her cheeks. Abruptly, she turned and walked through her mother's front door.

NINETEEN

For Blossom Black, the days following her return from her rendezvous in Montego Bay were sick days. She had lost her desire for food, and she ended up spewing the small amounts that she did eat. After six weeks had gone by, she dialed long distance. Her mother answered.

"Mom, I am longing to see you."

"Then take a quick trip, honey ... I am longing to see you too."

"Not like that, Mom; I really want to see you ... I mean ... I want to talk with you, urgently."

"What's the matter, hon ... Why do you want to talk with me urgently?"

Margareta Black was an experienced woman; she sensed that the matter was serious.

"Tell me honey, what's wrong?" Margareta coaxed Blossom in a low voice.

"Mom, I'm scared. I've not been keeping well for several weeks now, everything I eat turns my stomach and I've been taking too many days off from work ... I'm scared to go see the doctor, Mom. I fear he may tell me I have a dreadful disease."

Margareta Black laughed softly. "Bloss," she said, her voice was calm, "your illness has a name ... It's called morning sickness, and such an illness is associated with women who are with child ... You're expecting a baby, honey." Her mother's quiet laughter relieved Blossom.

"Mom, I'm sorry."

"You're sorry honey?" her mother asked in a loving tone. In her heart, Margareta Black knew her daughter would do whatever she wanted to do, in her own way, regardless of the consequences. She'd always been that way, no use in scolding her.

"I love you, honey," Margareta said.

"I love you too, Mom."

Blossom deliberated.

"Mom," ... she continued.

"What is it honey"? Margareta asked.

"Mom ... I have your beautiful eyes, and I'm shaped like you, I am definitely my mother's daughter."

"Indeed honey... and yet, you are your Daddy's girl, in so many ways."

Margareta Black sighed. She knew that her

daughter's beauty was her greatest asset—the envy of women and men alike. She knew that Blossom used her beauty whenever she needed to. She knew her daughter was capable of making men commit vile sins. Deep in Margareta Black's heart, she knew that her daughter had inherited Whitfield Black's superb DNA.

At first, Blossom didn't want to believe she had conceived the child she'd wished for, but after a quick pharmacy test and a second test to confirm, she was sure she was with child. She wanted to tell her sister Odette the news, but she was scared. She knew Odette would not be as sympathetic as her mother had been.

She was terrified to go to work, certain that her regular barfing in the ladies room would reveal her secret. She was too ashamed to look Seymour Johnson in the eyes, and she avoided Ron Johnson as if she had an infectious disease.

Blossom was practical. She knew that having a child out of wedlock was risky and an enormous stigma may be attached to the child's illegitimate status. But she was financially stable and she was certain she could manage.

Maybe I will take up residence in a faraway city. Calgary, maybe in Vancouver, be anonymous, Blossom thought. Then she would not have to deal with the shame that people would heap on her, but she remembered how much she wanted to bear Sheldon's child and she said aloud, "No amount of shame—nothing or no one—will make me go into hiding."

"Your cold's been hanging around too long, Blossom, have you been checked out by a doctor?" Ron was concerned when he phoned to see how she had been keeping.

"Really Ron, my cold sounds much worse than it is, I'll see you at the office on Monday."

Monday came. Blossom knocked on Ron's office door and entered. She knew there was no easy way to tell Ron the truth, she would just let the truth come out in its own way: She didn't have a cold—she was expecting a child.

"Welcome back, Blossom. How's your cold?" Ron was sporting a wide smile.

Blossom was straight-faced.

"My cold is better. Thank you, Ron," she answered politely.

"Then why the poker face?" Ron laughed.

"I am expecting a baby," Blossom said in a listless tone. Ron smiled a bashful smile.

"So it isn't a cold after all?" He was moved by the revelation. "We are having a baby? ... Oh boy ... The two of us will soon make three? That's good news, sweetheart. Let's take a week off and go somewhere, get married ... Have a honeymoon?"

Ron was beside himself with glee. He walked over to Blossom and pulled her gently to him. "Blossom,

I'm elated."

Blossom went limp in his arms.

"Ron, I'm sorry to tell you this, the baby I'm carrying is not your baby." Ron pulled back.

"What the hell did you just say Blossom?" He looked at her with narrowed eyes. Suddenly, Blossom felt ill at ease, she slumped in the oversize armchair in Ron's office.

"I'm sorry Ron; I had to tell the truth."

"You had to tell me the truth? Do you think the truth will make me feel better? Fuck it! Whose baby are you carrying, if not mine?" Ron was mad as hell.

Blossom didn't speak.

Ron thought for a moment.

"It's that idiot son-of-a-bitch in Montego Bay you call Sheldon, isn't it?" Ron said at a pitch much louder than Blossom had ever heard.

"It's him, isn't it?" Ron repeated with contempt and ridicule.

Ron Johnson knew enough to peg Sheldon Morgan as the man responsible. When Blossom said nothing, Ron carried on, he was stark raving mad.

"That mother fucker ... wherever he is, I'm going to hunt him down and pound the son-of-a-bitch to a bloody pulp ... and, how the hell can you be sure that you're not carrying my child? I need a strong drink," Ron barked, one hand on his hip and the other touching his forehead.

Blossom moved quickly to the liquor drawer and fixed Ron a double scotch on ice; he drank some, and then spewed out the rest through his gritted teeth. Blossom wiped up the spill.

"Ron, I simply was not thinking responsibly ... I made an irrational decision, I'm very sorry. I admit, very often I've rushed off to Montego Bay and lied about the reason I go there ... I'm truly sorry ... Can you forgive me?"

Ron took another gulp of his scotch and threw the rest against the wall. Splatters trickled down, simultaneous with the tears that rolled down Blossom cheeks.

"Forgive? ... Blossom you fucked the son-of-a-bitch, and he knocked you up, now you want me to forgive you? Forgive?" Ron repeated the word several times as he paced around his office, pounding his fists on every vacant space on the wall.

Blossom's tears kept on coming. She never thought that it would've been so tough when the truth came out.

"I'll see you at your apartment tonight, at seven o'clock," Ron was furious.

"As you wish, Ron," Blossom replied.

When Blossom arrived home, she quickly put away the dishes and fluffed the cushions.

Ron might arrive at seven o'clock. She expected he may well be on time, as he was a punctual man.

She reached for the phone on the kitchen wall to call Ron. He might still be at the office. She wanted to tell him not to come—not tonight but she put the phone back in its cradle. Why call Ron now?

She was restless; this visit would be unlike the relaxing afternoons they'd regularly spent over drinks or hot cups of tea. She checked to see that there was enough of his favorite drink in the decanter. Suddenly the intercom in her suite rang.

"Concierge, Miss Black ... Mr. Johnson is here."

Ron had arrived early.

"Send him up, Freddie."

Blossom opened the door to Ron. He was still wearing his business suit and tie. She kissed him on both cheeks; strong scent of whiskey was still on his breath. "Hello, my love, how are you feeling?"

"A lot better, thank you." Blossom answered politely.

Ron walked into the solarium. He looked out at the starlit sky, "It's a lovely evening, let's go out for salmon dinner."

"Not tonight, Ron ... I have no appetite for salmon," Blossom responded.

Ron sat beside Blossom on the love seat and put an arm around her.

"Sweetheart, I'm sorry about our spat today. I was out of control; please forgive me."

"You had every reason to be out of control, Ron. I'm the one who need your forgiveness," Blossom turned and looked at him; she realized her situation was as hard for Ron to understand, as it would be for her to explain. Ron Johnson had invested many years in his relationship with Blossom and she understood that she owed him an enormous amount of respect.

"Ron, may I say something?"

"You want to say something ... Now?"

"Yes. May I?" Blossom asked softly.

Ron gave her a half smile.

"Only if you fix me my favorite drink."

She brought him his favorite mix of cognac.

"I thought about the consequences of my actions and I've made a decision that will make me feel a lot better about myself ... I've decided to step down from my position at the firm ... I'll also end our relationship. It would not be right for me to let my unprofessional behavior create negative chatter about you and the firm." Blossom sighed. "I will not tarnish your father's reputation. I'll relinquish my position effective four weeks from today."

Ron gulped the entire contents of his glass.

"Damn and blast it, Blossom ... I cannot let you move out of my life this way, we're partners. You're an asset to me and the firm. We've been together for a long time. We'll be husband and wife. Marry me, Blossom; I'll make you and the baby happy. This baby belongs to me ... I'm claiming this baby."

Blossom was silent. She was taken aback by the authority in Ron's voice.

"We've been good together, Sweetheart," Ron went on, "We've had the most satisfying sex with the protection of your birth control pills, so what if the pills let us down once. I don't fault you ... we'll be married."

"But that's not how it happened, Ron, the pills

didn't let us down, I wanted to have his child. Now I'm ready to face the consequences."

"Consequences? I have no concerns, marry me now Blossom." She kissed him.

"Tell me Blossom, tell me again, tell me you truly want to end our relationship, tell me until I believe you." Ron's tone suggested it would not be easy to break-up their relationship.

I love you, Ron Johnson. I love you, because you are a decent man; I love you, because you are the part of my memory that I'll always enjoy. I'm sorry, I messed up. I knew you'd want to make things right for me, but I don't deserve your love, and although I beg for your forgiveness, I don't deserve it. Please let me go, Ron; please don't try to hold me back ... Please, Ron, please ... Let me go.

The words did not come out; instead, Blossom whispered.

"I couldn't live with the guilt this situation will bring both of us. My situation has placed a barrier between us, and I'd rather not cross that barrier. I've already hurt other people; allow me to make changes that I can live with, changes that will make me feel whole again."

Ron brushed tears from Blossom's cheeks.

"Blossom, please don't leave me now... please re-consider your decision."

Blossom shuddered. Ron cradled her gently. They could not control their desires. They made passionate love, one more time.

When Ron said goodbye, Blossom quietly walked

into her solarium, she looked down at the busy freeway with introspection. Headlights were flickering and movement was continuous. For everyone else, nothing seemed to change, for Blossom Black, her life with Ron Johnson had just ended.

PART TWO

1987 – 2002

Your soul is oftentimes a battlefield, upon which your reason and your judgment wage war against your passion and your appetite.
And think not you can direct the course of love, for love, if it finds you worthy, directs your course.

—*Kahlil Gibran*, The Prophet

TWENTY

Blossom had been sitting in her favorite high back chair, gazing reflectively at her much loved paintings. She especially liked the Portrait called: *Woman*, by Escoffrey.

She selected a red rosebud from the flower arrangement on her coffee table. She twisted the stem as she contemplated her assets.

Her suite at The Emerald Place was sufficiently comfortable; her savings and investments were enough to sustain her and her child until she was ready to return to the workforce; she owned a mid-size sedan and she had invested in fine art and collectibles that would increase in value. Life with her child would be beautiful. Four more weeks at the firm was all the time she needed to wrap things up.

When Blossom hinted to Ruby Snipes that she was with child, Ruby's response sounded somewhat cynical. "Well, that's a surprise," she had said.

"I'm surprise too, Ruby; I thought I had entered menopause."

"So, what are you going to do, Miss Black?"

"Oh, I am going to have my baby."

"Congratulations! You are a lucky woman. How old are you … thirty-four?"

"Thirty-seven."

"Thirty-seven years old and you are having your first child?" Ruby shook her head.

"I wish I had a child of my own," she said.

Blossom had phoned David Clark as he'd asked of her, when she returned to Toronto from Montego Bay and David had let on that he was searching for a trademark and patent firm to do some work for his Marble and Granite Company in Ocho Rios.

"… And you'll meet with me to discuss the matter?" David had asked Blossom.

"I would be glad to." Blossom had answered.

David Clark was open about his success.

"I'm a self-made millionaire; I work very hard to accumulate my wealth. But my wife Clara may not be around long enough to enjoy the fruits of my labor." David talked about his wife's battle with lung cancer and considered it a terrible blow to his family. There seemed to be no limit to his love for his wife. Blossom was impressed. She showed empathy by telling David how she had lost her father to liver cancer and how hurtful it had been for her.

The phone on Blossom's desk rang. She recognized the caller to be David Clark.

"Hello Mr. Clark ... May I help you?"

"Hello ... Blossom, how have you been?"

"I've been well, thank you."

"I'm calling to confirm our meeting."

"Yes, yes ... we'll meet here in the boardroom at eleven o'clock."

"Great ... may I invite you to lunch with me after our meeting?"

"Thank you ... I would love that very much."

"Then we'll have lunch at the Old Mill Restaurant at two o'clock?"

"Very well." Blossom welcomed the change of pace which included lunch with David Clark

The Old Mill was a lovely country-style banquet facility, decorated in 19th century flair that bordered on a ravine in an enclave at the foot of Toronto. It was the ideal place for lunch. David Clark was seated at a private table in the dining room when Blossom arrived. He waved a hand and called out.

"Over here, Blossom."

He pulled out a cushioned chair from under the circular table and offered Blossom a seat. When they were comfortably seated, the waiter appeared. He smiled respectfully at David.

"Felix ... I'll have the red snapper, steamed. The lady will have grilled Fillet of Sole." It was evident that David had been a regular client.

"I have to say I am pleased with the outcome of our meeting this morning," David smiled at Blossom "... And your recommendations are well taken ... Please proceed with patent and trademark for granite and marble separately."

"Very well Mr. Clark," Blossom smiled.

Blossom ate a small portion of her meal then she put her fork down. David was concerned that she had not eaten enough.

"Really Mr. Clark, I am full," she said, smiling.

"When we last spoke your wife had just been out of the hospital, how has she been keeping?" Blossom asked,

David dabbed the corners of his mouth with his table napkin, "Clara succumbed two weeks ago." Suddenly David looked sad.

"I am very sorry Mr. Clark, you must be hurting."

"I loved Clara very much ... I'm missing her. I have my two daughters and life goes on." David was clearly putting on a bold face. He drew in a long deep breath.

"We had a wonderful life together," David looked sideways as if to hide a tear; then he took a sip from his cup; "So, what's new with you?" He was curious but polite.

"I am going to be a mother, Mr. Clark."

"You're expecting a baby?"

"Yes, in August," Blossom answered excitedly.

"Congratulations my dear." David turned a boyish grin "... Forgive me for being inquisitive, Miss Black ... When did you get married?" He paused for a moment then he continued "... and who's the lucky guy?" he sounded eager.

Blossom put her teacup back in the saucer.

"I'm afraid I didn't get married."

"Oh ... Is everything going to be alright with you?" David asked, showing concern.

"Yes ... Yes ... Sheldon loves me although he and I live in different worlds."

Blossom was vague.

"Sheldon?" David made furrows on his forehead.

"Yes ... Sheldon Morgan ... We were together in Montego Bay last November."

Blossom inhaled deeply.

David scratched his head.

"Does Sheldon know he's going to be a father?"

"Not yet."

David paused for a moment.

"But you *will* tell him ... right?"

"Not likely ... I will not make this child an issue."

David hesitated. "The child will be an issue whether you like it or not."

David sounded like a big brother, perhaps an uncle or a godfather. Blossom suddenly felt queasy, she picked up her clutch purse and tucked it under her arm.

David signaled the waiter to bring the check. He paid with a generous tip.

Blossom and David exited the Old Mill; the smell of freshly baked bread enticed Blossom's maternity cravings.

What will I name my baby, she thought as David settled her in her car.

"Jason, that's it. Jason Sheldon Black, will be the name of my child," Blossom said aloud.

David looked at her, curiously. "You're having a boy?"

"Yes." Blossom answered with a smile.

TWENTY-ONE

Ron stared blankly out the window. His mind was set on Blossom Black, the woman who caught his eyes on that fateful morning ten years before. She had been a competent, mature executive in his firm. He had fallen in love with her and now, with her exit, he felt like his personal life was falling apart.

The rain had started late that afternoon. Heavy drops beat outside the wide windowpane of Ron's 14th floor office. His first thought was to spend the chilly afternoon having a warm cup of tea with Blossom. But that was not to be, she'd left him three months before.

Ron never thought it was wise to develop a relationship with any of the ladies at the firm but with Blossom Black, he rolled the dice.

"You are smart as you are beautiful," Ron had said to Blossom one time when she closed an uncertain deal for the firm.

Ron admitted his fascination with beautiful Blossom Black overtook his life in a remarkable way. He wondered whether anything or anyone would ever fill the empty space in his heart, created by her exit.

For Ron, the luxury of working and playing with an eye-catching and bright woman like Blossom was an extravagance he relished and he had seriously considered making her his wife.

He reached for the phone on his desk. He dialed. He had dialed those numbers many times before. The answering machine clicked on, *you have reached Blossom Black ... sorry I'm unable to answer this call ...* Ron hung up and crossed the hall to Seymour Johnson's office.

"Dad, please send a different lawyer to represent Donna Graham in her Sexual Harassment matter."

"You no longer wish to handle the Graham file? What's troubling you, son?"

"I'm not focused Dad," Ron said, shaking his head from side to side.

"How has Miss Black been these days?" Seymour Johnson inquired, sensing his son's sadness.

"She doesn't take my calls. Dad, I miss her. When I sleep, she's in my dreams, when I'm awake I wonder if she's alright. My days are not the same since she's been gone ... I'm literally lost without her."

Seymour Johnson gazed intently at Ron, he could

not guarantee any advice to his lovelorn son.

"There is someone else in her life, Dad."

"She admitted this to you?"

"Common sense ... I proposed marriage to her more than once and each time she'd asked me to wait; now she's carrying *his* child." Ron was clearly annoyed.

"Say hello to her for me," Seymour Johnson was at a loss for words.

"I'll be in the rotunda, smoking a cigarette," Ron said and exited his father's office.

Blossom closed the book she'd been reading. She looked down at rush-hour traffic from her solarium. Thoughts about happier times at the firm played in her memory even though she'd tried hard to keep them at bay. Blossom had spoken to Ruby Snipes her former assistant, mostly to tie off loose ends.

"I'll be glad to help you out with chores when the little one arrives," Ruby had volunteered.

Ron had phoned several times. Blossom had wondered if he would ever stop calling. She picked up the phone on the coffee table and dialed Ron's number. Ron answered immediately. "Hello?"

"It's Blossom, how are you Ron?" Blossom inquired politely.

"Missing you sweetheart... how are *you*? Did you receive my messages?"

"I'm well ... yes, I received your messages. Please accept my apologies for the delay in returning the calls."

"Apologies are unnecessary, Blossom, I've been calling to know if you're fine, to see if there's something I can do for you. I'd love to meet with you, for lunch maybe? You, me and the baby ... Your choice of restaurant."

"You're very kind, Ron. The baby and I regret we have to decline."

Ron persisted. "I was hoping we'd have a conversation about reuniting—getting back together. Damn it Blossom, I miss you."

"Parting is tough, I miss you too."

"Ron, you asked me to rethink my decision. Let me explain, I ended our relationship for the reasons I told you before, I cannot pretend that I conceived your child ... I cannot do that. Please understand, my mind is made up." Ron was devastated.

"My life has changed since you've been gone Blossom ... I know I'll never be the same. It will be hard to live without you ..." Ron paused, "Dad has asked me to give you his best wishes."

Blossom was silent.

"Blossom? Blossom are you there?" Sheldon asked as the silence at the other end of the phone persisted.

"Please give Seymour my regards. Goodbye Ron." Blossom responded. She felt fresh tears coming down and she quickly clicked away.

Ron had wished for Blossom to come back to him. He dialed his father.

"Dad, meet me at the *Lawyers Bench* in the Hilton Hotel for a drink."

"I'll meet you there, son," Seymour Johnson breathed a sigh of relief.

That afternoon, Ron had been in his office preparing for a Court appearance the next day. He'd tried to focus on the task at hand but he couldn't and he knew why—all manner of thoughts had clouded his mind and all of them were associated with Blossom. He walked over to the window and looked down at the landscape from the 14th floor. His jaw tightened. He had hoped his second attempt at love would've been lifelong, but it was good while it lasted. He inhaled a deep breath.

"It'll be a very long time before I recover from this disappointment," he said aloud.

Ron pulled his chair up to his desk. He wrote.

My darling Bloss,

Do not, for a moment think I will accept your retreat from my life for I will love you as long as I live. I always knew your heart belonged to someone else but somehow I thought the gods would've been kinder to me.

Memories of you will be forever stamped in my mind—the way you scolded me when I crossed a forbidden line, the way you pursed your lips when you were in deep concentration and the way your body sealed mine in tender moments. These memories are what sustain me these days. Know that I'll forever love you. Ron.

TWENTY-TWO

David Clark stayed close to Blossom during her prenatal period. He had been exceedingly attentive to her. Not that she was bothered. David was a kind, fatherly man, perhaps he'd been the same way with his daughters.

Blossom and David depended on each other. David to mitigate the pain from the loss of his wife of 29 years, and Blossom, to dull the ache that never subsided after her breakaway from Ron Johnson and the firm. Ruby Snipes, Blossom's former assistant. had been missing her, Ruby visited Blossom often.

Blossom decided against telling Sheldon Morgan he had fathered her child, she wanted to be confident when the time was right for such a disclosure. For now, she accepted that she would be on her own.

Two weeks before her delivery, Blossom and David stopped for lunch at The Farmer's House, a cozy restaurant at the rim of Queen Street in the picturesque town of Streetsville.

They found their favorite spot by the fireplace in the main dining room and stayed for a while to enjoy the music. The atmosphere was tranquil.

Blossom suddenly noticed the gray that had started at David's temples. His dignified manner showed a man still grieving the loss of his wife.

David picked up on Blossom's frame of mind. He slowly put down his glass of wine and pushed it off to the side. He slid both hands across the table, lightly touching Blossom's wrists.

"Life is short and very unpredictable ... let's get married ... that way I can legitimately take care of you and the baby," David said.

"Let's get married, Blossom," he repeated, perhaps making sure Blossom heard what he had said.

"I don't know, David ... I never thought of you in that way."

"I've always thought of you in that way ... I just wasn't sure you would accept me ... If I'd told you I admired you from the first time I saw you, would you have believed me?" David paused, took a deep breath and continued, "I admire your ways ... I want to be with you all the time ... you make me very happy, Blossom ... just watching you grow and expand makes me want to be a new father."

Blossom studied David carefully "David, I can't."

As if reading Blossom's mind, David said, "I never thought I'd ask another woman to marry me so soon after Clara, please consider my proposal.

Blossom deliberated, David would be a good husband and the perfect father for her child but she feared that his motivation might be to shield her from embarrassment. Like Ron Johnson, David might feel it an obligation to rescue and protect her.

"I'm not asking you to marry me immediately because of pity for you, I'm not even trying to own you," David continued "I *can* make you and the baby happy Blossom … you and the baby *will* make me happy."

"I want you to be happy, David."

"Would you consider a trial marriage?" David asked. Blossom thought for a moment, she'd always wanted to be who *she* wanted to be, the thought of *belonging* to someone made her nervous, now she was willing to admit, if only to herself, that her fear of marriage had not been good for her. David Clark was a wise man; he gave Blossom a reasonable alternative. She smiled.

"A trial marriage could work."

"I had to have you, one way or another," David laughed heartily. "Now I'll tell my daughters about the arrangement. It might not be too difficult for Dana to accept, being married and settled herself, Camille still lives in the family home, and she's surrounded by things that remind her about her mother, she might not be ready for a step-mother."

Blossom was matter-of-fact, "I agree, it might be difficult for Camille to accept me so soon."

"I did approve of her living in the North York home with her fiancé Peter Grange ... Peter seems like a solid young man ... he will help to settle Camille ... they will be married next June."

"I'm happy for them David," Blossom smiled.

David was pragmatic in many ways; he did not oppose the idea when Blossom suggested that in the event Sheldon Morgan became aware of his child, no barriers would be placed in his way.

"Your suite at The Emerald Place ... is there enough room for the three of us," David enquired.

"Oh yes, more than enough," she answered.

"Take a look at those homes in the town of Milton, Blossom," David suggested. "Milton is an expanding town; the area is quiet and easily accessible to other towns. My colleague Bob Cousins built some beautiful homes out there," David went on. Blossom smiled and said, "I've heard about the town of Milton, I've actually looked at residences in Milton but I come back to The Emerald Place ... I love The Emerald Place."

Blossom's delivery date was approaching, she'd been checking off the items she should pack for her delivery. The baby's nursery was prepared and decorated in pastel blue with a touch of pastel yellow and pink. Plush teddy bears and toys were in place to add to the beauty of the room and a qualified babysitter was reserved to look after Jason during intervals when Blossom needed a break. Everything was ready for Jason's arrival.

Odette had been counting down the days. "I want to be there with you, Bloss; would you like me to come?" The sisters have always been protective of each other. "You will be *here* with me in spirit, Odie" Blossom said after a reflective pause.

Margareta phoned with daily instructions and lessons on motherhood. "Be sure to breastfeed the baby Bloss ... nothing is better than the mother's milk for your baby," she told Blossom

David was enjoying the feel of the baby's movement. Blossom was healthy and glowing.

If she had been embarrassed or ashamed because of her unmarried pregnancy, that was no longer the case.

TWENTY-THREE

Dr. Bradford had asked for Blossom to be admitted into Queen's Hospital a week early just in case she needed to deliver by cesarean section. David was ready for the task. His lessons in Lamaze were useful when delivery pains came. "C-section will be a last resort for me," Blossom had told David.

"She's been in a lot of pain, Dr. Bradford." David was concerned.

"Our medical team will monitor her situation carefully, Mr. Clark," Dr. Bradford assured David.

When the baby kept still David inquired if it was time to consider cesarean section, Dr. Bradford decided it was time. "Let's do it now." Dr. Bradford said. The surgery was successful. Blossom was glad that David was not squeamish.

"Congratulations! You delivered a boy," Dr. Bradford was beaming. David Clark stood by the side of Blossom's bed with a broad smile. He was happy. He pointed to a bouquet of flowers on her bedside table. "The flowers are from staff at the office," David was smiling.

A bundle was placed beside Blossom and she was wheeled to her private room for recovery.

Shortly after Jason's arrival, Margareta Black came up from Montego Bay to visit her daughter and grandson for two weeks.

"Jason looks so much like his grand-daddy." Margareta said.

Blossom was grateful that her mother took over Jason's care during her visit. The realization that her father was no longer alive to see the grandchild he'd always wanted made Blossom sad. All the same, Blossom was happy that Jason had some of his granddaddy's features.

Four-week-old Jason was swaddled and tucked in Blossom's arms, sound asleep. She had been in the solarium going over a list of invitees to Jason's baptism. David walked in.

"What're you doing, honey," he kissed Blossom on her cheek.

"I am completing the guest list for Jason's baptism," Blossom answered.

David gently lifted Jason out of Blossom's arms and kissed him.

"Darling, be sure to invite Ken and Kathleen, I

would love to have Ken as my best man."

Blossom turned around sharply "... a best man? At a baptism?" her forehead crinkled.

"Absolutely ... Let's get married on the day of Jason's baptism ... that way Father Templeton can *kill* two birds with one stone," David was serious.

Blossom had not yet said yes to David's marriage proposal. She realized such a question required an honest and straightforward answer. She considered the muddle she'd made of her personal life and she decided that David, being the experienced man he'd been, would be ideal for her. She no longer wished to play the game of *give me more time*.

"Sure, honey, I will send two invitations to Ken and Kathleen, one for our wedding and one for Jason's baptism ... We'll do the two ceremonies on the same day."

"I'll phone Ken and demand that he be my best man." David laughed.

"Ken and Kathleen might be in Seattle around the time of Jason's baptism visiting their new grandchild," Blossom reminded David.

"Then we'll rearrange our date ... I won't give Ken a free pass," David laughed.

Blossom sat back in her chair and watched David cuddle Jason in a tender way. There and then she was convinced she had made the right decision to marry David Clark.

On their wedding day and Jason's baptism, Blossom pulled her hair back in a bun at the nape of her neck. The neckline of her beautifully designed form-fitting calf length dress plunged in the back with tiny looped buttons in a straight line that rested at the ridge of her buttocks. She wore beige sling-back shoes with a matching clutch purse. The diamond-studded bracelet that David had given her for a wedding present looked magnificent on her left wrist.

David was dapper in his dark gray tuxedo with gorgeous satin bands running down the outer legs of his suit pants. Blossom hooked David's gold cuff links into his crisp white shirt sleeves and smiled.

Father Templeton pronounced David Olson Clark and Blossom Mae Black, man and wife on the day they baptized their son Jason.

Love had found David and Blossom in a very special way. After the ceremonies David kissed Blossom lightly on her lips, she smiled, knowing that her life had taken an unexpected turn.

Father Templeton and his wife were among forty invited guests at the wedding reception.

David's best man, Ken Daley, stood and raised his champagne glass; "David Clark," he said, "You're a fortunate man—you're healthy, you're wealthy, you're complete. And today, we all join in wishing you a blissful married life with your beautiful bride." The guests burst out in a round of applause.

Father Templeton sang: *Now that we've found Love,* a beautiful reggae song made popular by the group *Third World.* His wife backed him up on her rhythm guitar. David was all smiles. The evening was perfect.

Hours later, when Blossom and David were in their honeymoon suite at the Royal York Hotel and Jason tucked in his crib, David took Blossom in his arms. "I love you Blossom … just knowing that you accepted my love makes me very happy." He hooked a twelve-inch strand pearl necklace around Blossom's neck and kissed her. "Let's continue our celebrations with a glass of Dom Perignon champagne, Mrs. Clark," David whispered.

"That we will, Mr. Clark," Blossom replied.

TWENTY-FOUR

Jason was in a hurry to grow up. At three months old, he was lifting his head when he heard sounds, holding on to fingers, rolling over and moving about on his back. He was an active, healthy baby.

When Jason came down with a cold, Blossom knew that he was producing an early tooth, she was ecstatic; and she was not alarmed about the slight temperature that accompanied the cold.

"Jason still has a slight temperature," she'd said to David when he called from the office to confirm their usual Friday evening dinner date.

"So you want us to cancel our date tonight?"

"No, no," Blossom answered quickly. "Mona will be sitting with him as usual."

David agreed.

By the time Mona arrived to sit with Jason he was sleeping. Blossom gave Mona instructions about Jason's medicine doses and the times they were due. Then she kissed Jason goodnight and scooted off.

The descending elevator stopped on the 10th floor and a woman wearing jogging outfit hopped in.

"Hi, my name is Lorna; I'm new at this address."

"Hi Lorna, my name is Blossom, I'm pleased to meet you. Welcome to The Emerald Place, I hope you'll enjoy living here."

The two women chatted as the elevator descended to the lobby.

"You are beautiful," David said when Blossom stepped out of the elevator wearing a pastel yellow dress. He gently pulled the matching shawl close to her shoulders and ushered her into their car. Blossom took several deep breaths of the cool November wind before she settled in the passenger seat.

Couples walked along the sidewalk and children played as parents kept a watchful eye on them. It was a beautiful night.

Blossom and David arrived at their favorite Italian restaurant in Port Credit. Gino, the suave host seated them at their usual table near the fireplace.

Gino was familiar with their dinner routine, he handed the menu to David.

"Will you be having your usual dinner tonight, Mrs. Clark?" The waiter looked at Blossom.

"I'll have Lasagna Verde with mozzarella cheese sprinkled on top ... thank you," Blossom's replied.

Their dinner conversation was light, mainly about events of the past week. They clearly enjoyed each other's company.

At the end of dinner and a glass of white wine David dabbed the corners of his mouth with his dinner napkin and said, "We'd better get back early to tend to Jason." He wrapped Blossom's shawl snuggly around her shoulders and guided her out of the restaurant.

When Blossom and David arrived back at The Emerald Place, the area was buzzing with emergency activity. An ambulance, a fire truck and two police cars waited in the circle around Tower 2. Emergency lights were flashing and people were milling about in the courtyard. Blossom was curious, she turned a puzzled look at David, "Could it be a fire drill?"

"Doesn't look that way ... a fire drill is orderly and without emergency responders," David replied.

Lorna, the woman whom Blossom had met in the elevator earlier pushed her way through the front door, "What's going on Blossom?" she inquired.

"Don't know." Blossom answered and briskly walked into the open elevator door, at the side of the concierge booth.

"The elevators are temporarily out of service, ma'am," the concierge looked at Blossom as she and David waited inside the open elevator door for it to close.

"We'd like to go up to our suite on the Twenty-first floor," Blossom explained.

"Sorry ma'am, no one is allowed on the twenty-first floor ... except the police; there has been an emergency."

Blossom looked closely at the guard; he wasn't Freddie the regular guard.

"An emergency? What happened?"

The guard paused. "Ma'am, you best speak to this police officer ... he'll tell you."

Blossom became annoyed.

"You sir, must not know who I am ... my name is Blossom Black ... I live in suite 2108," Blossom was at that point screaming.

"Blossom Black? 2108? Please come with me," The guard said. David grabbed Blossom's arm, "Is something wrong?"

"Sir, Ma'am, this way please." a police officer said.

Blossom and David moved to follow the police officer. All of a sudden they saw a covered stretcher being pushed out of an elevator by two attendants. Mona followed closely. The attendants hoisted the stretcher into the open rear doors of an ambulance. Blossom hopped in before the doors closed. Jason was on the stretcher and a paramedic was hunched over him. Mona was holding Jason's little hand. Something had gone terribly wrong. The ambulance sped away.

Blossom and David paced the floor in the hospital lounge as they await word about Jason.

Dr. Moore appeared in green scrubs and a green mask hanging under her chin. She touched Blossom's shoulders gently and escorted her and David to an adjacent room. David's grip tightened around Blossom's fingers.

"I'm sorry ..."

"Why is Dr. Moore saying she is sorry? My baby ... he is alright ... isn't he?" Blossom looked deep into David's eyes.

Dr. Moore remained silent for a moment.

"SIDS happens without warning," Dr. Moore said.

"SIDS? What is SIDS? My baby is healthy."

"SIDS is Sudden Infant Death Syndrome... also known as crib death ... it is not a disease, Mrs. Clark...you're correct, Jason was a healthy baby ... SIDS happens with no warning signs or clear reason in babies up to a year old... likely, Jason had been sleeping on his stomach at the time."

Blossom fainted.

She woke up later in a hospital bed and looked around in surprise—why was she in a hospital.

"Jason," Blossom cried out.

A nurse gave her pills and a glass of water and she drifted off to sleep.

When she woke up again, David was leaning over her bed. "Thank heavens, you are alright," he said.

"Where's my baby ... I want my baby," Blossom screamed.

A nurse gave her more pills and water.

David was touched by Blossom's weeping and hollering. He understood her needed to cry and he waited patiently while she cried.

* * *

Friends wandered in and out of suite 2108. David sat beside Blossom on the loveseat with a comforting arm around her shoulders. Mrs. Mullins stood by the window looking down at traffic whisking back and forth on the freeway.

"God knows best," Mrs. Mullins remarked.

"Not now, Mrs. Mullins," Blossom said as she held her belly and cried. She thought she felt birth pains all over again. David was distraught.

"We'll go away on a holiday after this is over Blossom."

"David," Blossom screamed ... "How dare you say we'll go away on a holiday, I cannot go on a holiday without my baby ... I want my baby back." Blossom screamed at the top of her lungs.

"I want my baby," Blossom cried repeatedly.

"Give me your pain, honey ... I'll ease your pain," David said. "I might not be able to give you another baby but I can ease your pain."

Blossom sank her face into David's shoulders. "I want our baby back," she bawled.

TWENTY-FIVE
Montego Bay

"I will not see a marriage counselor," Sheldon said to his wife Maureen during an intense argument. Things had not been going well between them, and each time they debated the state of their marriage, he threw the miscarriage of their child on her like a wet towel.

"Maureen, your revelation about our expected child did not pan out. Damn it, Mo, you lied to me."

"That was not a lie, Sheldon ... I *was* carrying our child," Maureen paused, "I think I know what this is about, it is about Blossom Black ... Why do you still care for her?" Without waiting for Sheldon to reply, Maureen continued, "You still dream about her ... don't you?"

"What're you talking about?" Sheldon asked.

"You know what I'm talking about—you know that

Blossom Black is in your dreams."

"No, I'm too busy with work."

"You work too hard ... Let's take a vacation."

"You have a place in mind?"

"Niagara Falls ... I've always wanted to see Niagara Falls."

Niagara Falls sounded like a fine place to go on a vacation. Sheldon liked the idea and smiled at Maureen. "Okay, Niagara Falls it is."

Maureen walked over and threw her arms around Sheldon's neck, happy that her suggestion made him smile—a vacation in Niagara Falls might be the fresh start their struggling marriage needed.

When Sheldon and Maureen arrived in Toronto, en route to Niagara Falls for their vacation, his first thought was to inform Blossom that he was in town. He expected that her response to him might be halfhearted, for he had not spoken with her since he had last seen her a year earlier. But he was actually longing to see her even if his wife had to be part of the get-together.

Sheldon picked up a payphone at the airport in Toronto. Several rings later, he recognized Blossom's voice at the other end.

"Hello, Bloss ... How are you?" He realized immediately how casual his greeting had been, but he couldn't think of a better way to break the ice and start a conversation. There was a heavy pause.

What followed was Blossom's chilling revelation about the death of her son whom he supposedly fathered. What's more, he learned that the child was only three months old at death.

"For goodness sakes Bloss ...You should've told me you were carrying my child!" Sheldon said.

"I never wanted this child to be an issue," Blossom replied.

The revelation was crushing, Sheldon paused for a moment, he wasn't sure if there was a role for him to play. He requested to see Blossom that same afternoon and she agreed.

I ought to phone my project manager to be sure that all is well on the sites, Sheldon said to himself. He dialed: "Dixon, this is Sheldon how are things?"

"Glad you called boss...not entirely good..."

Sheldon stood by the phone on the wall and contemplated the sudden turn of events. Then he returned to the spot where Maureen had been waiting for him. He looked at her apologetically.

"We have to return to Montego Bay tomorrow on the first flight we get."

"Something is wrong?"

"Trouble at the West Hill project ... The guys at Wilbrothers Construction up at West Hill walked off the job in a wildcat strike this morning ... They've stormed my site looking for work ... Doug Williams is threatening to cause trouble if Dixon hires any of Wilbrothers' men ... This could turn ugly."

"What do we do now?"

"We stay at the Holiday Inn near here tonight ... then we get cracking back to Montego Bay as early as possible tomorrow."

Maureen knew better than to make any suggestion that would discourage Sheldon from canceling their vacation. More than anything, Sheldon was determined to see Blossom straightaway.

Sheldon arrived at Blossom's suite dressed in a dark suit and tie with a small box in his hand. His frame filled the doorway. He surveyed the sparsely lit living room. People were moving about and the smell of burnt logs was in the air.

Sheldon's eyes appeared dark with what Blossom made out to be grief. His somber expression sent a shudder through her body. She felt an urge to run to him, hold him tight and listen to the beat of his strong heart.

Sheldon paused for a moment to look at the large portrait of Jason at three months old that hung above the mantle. He studied the photograph. Blossom watched as his mouth went rigid and his shoulders stiffened. His lips moved but uttered no words. He raised his hands and pressed his index fingers against both of his ears, evidently blocking out sounds only he could hear.

Deliberately Sheldon crossed the floor to the far corner where Blossom had been standing with her arms folded. He attempted to get closer. She cringed and held up both her palms signaling him to stop. He moved back to the open front door, not knowing what his role ought to be. *She gave birth to my child*, Sheldon said to himself. Blossom inhaled deeply and let out a sigh. As if reading his mind, she whispered to herself, "I was selfish—I owe Sheldon an apology." But she didn't apologize even though David had cautioned her that it would be unfair if she kept the baby a secret. Blossom held Sheldon's gaze. She wondered how different it would've been if he'd known she was carrying his child. She walked to the front door where he stood.

"Why didn't you tell me you were expecting our child?" His voice was a mere whisper. His head bent to hide the glisten in his eyes. He attempted to touch her; he pulled back when he noticed the band on her finger. "Our love produced a son?" Sheldon whispered.

Blossom remained silent.

Sheldon looked deeply into Blossom's eyes; he felt sorry for their loss—the child had belonged to him also, he was certain of it. She looked away. She couldn't bear to see the look of despair in his eyes.

David Clark walked in; he seemed surprised if not annoyed to see Sheldon Morgan. He put an arm around Blossom's shoulders.

"Honey, are you alright?" he asked pressing her head against his chest.

Blossom nodded. She was thankful for the comfort of her husband.

"We've got to reach the church by two o'clock,"

David said to Blossom without acknowledging Sheldon's presence.

Sheldon leaned against Blossom's open front door with his hands in his pockets, likely recognizing the connection between her and David.

Blossom picked up her clutch purse, and walked out into the afternoon leaving Sheldon standing outside her door.

TWENTY-SIX

The weather forecast called for a bright and sunny afternoon but for Blossom, the skies were gray and the atmosphere was hazy. She was on her way to the small neighborhood chapel for Jason's funeral Mass. With her rosary wrapped around the palm of her right hand, she recited a prayer as she eased into her Mercedes-Benz. She wanted to be in the chapel before Mass started for a reflective moment.

With her eyes closed, Blossom knelt at the altar and quietly prayed. She felt a big warm hand on her shoulder and when she opened her eyes and looked up she recognized the face of Sheldon Morgan. His eyes were dark with grief; his shoulders hunched. He looked deep into her eyes and said nothing. She closed her eyes and in the silence of her heart, she continued to pray.

Dear God, I cannot stand to look into Sheldon's eyes at this moment. I cannot stand his grief and he cannot stand my grief. Father, please forgive us for we have sinned. Please forgive the hurt we've caused ourselves and others. Have mercy on our mortal soul, and give us strength to endure as we lay our child, your son, to rest.

When she stood up, Sheldon had been gazing at her. She wanted to tell him she was sorry but she didn't have the courage. She turned and walked to the front pew. Sheldon walked to the back of the Chapel and sat on a bench.

A tiny brass coffin was wheeled in. The mourners were arriving. Mass began.

Blossom listened in a daze as Father Templeton conducted the funeral rites. Mass was over in an hour. Burial followed.

"You need not stay for the burial," David said to Blossom and patted her hand. "You've endured enough."

"I shall see Jason off," Blossom said.

When Blossom turned and looked; her eyes met Sheldon's, he'd been sitting alone at the back of the empty chapel. His lips moved without sounds. Blossom shook her head from side to side, *Let him grieve*, she thought and continued to walk.

David took Blossom's elbow. He guided her to her car and closed the door quietly.

Sheldon walked slowly to his rental car, he considered he should return to the Holiday Inn where his wife Maureen had been waiting, but instead, he joined the procession for Jason's interment. "My son, my only child," tears streamed down Sheldon's cheek.

When Sheldon returned to the Holiday Inn, Maureen faced him.

"Honey, I was worried about you. Where have you been?"

"I attended a funeral."

"Someone you know?"

"Someone I never met; I wanted to pay my respects." Sheldon answered.

Maureen recognized that her husband had had a rough day; she did not want to be inquisitive so she left him alone.

Sheldon walked over to the big glass window in their room. He looked out to the freeway below. Maureen joined her husband.

"Have to go take care of business on the site," Sheldon said as though he were conversing with himself.

TWENTY-SEVEN

"Honey, I've already tied up all the loose ends, I've taken care of police inquiries and hospital reports, I've filled out all the necessary papers and I've arranged with Lorna Jones from the 10th floor to assist you with miscellaneous things in the meantime."

"I'm grateful to you for handling matters, honey," Blossom said.

"We'll meet our guests at Martel's at six o'clock, for Jason's reception ... did you tell Mr. Morgan he's welcome to join us?" David asked Blossom.

"No David ... I never thought to invite him."

It was just as well that Blossom did not invite

Sheldon; the pain would have been too much for the two of them. "We will invite him and his wife over for dinner before they return to Montego Bay," David suggested.

No, we won't, Blossom said inwardly.

Martel's was an old-fashioned Steakhouse at the bottom of Horner Avenue at Lakeshore Road. Friends and family gathered in the banquet hall to celebrate the life of Baby Jason.

After Father Templeton prayed over the meal, he gave a short address; "Baby Jason was only three months old … too young to be sad," Let's sing a happy song," he said.

Someone in the group belted out the popular rendition: *For he's a jolly good fellow* and everyone joined in and sang.

"Let's be happy. Baby Jason is gone to a better place," Father Templeton continued.

Blossom celebrated Jason's short life in silent contemplation. *Jason's conception and delivery were two of my greatest achievements* she said inwardly and sighed.

"You have not eaten your meal, my dear." David observed. "I'll be hungry soon, honey" Blossom assured David.

After the reception, they stopped at the neighborhood market for last minute purchases. David had been pushing the shopping cart ahead through the checkout line while Blossom lingered to check the coins she'd received from the cashier.

Suddenly she felt faint and unsteady. She held on to the pole beside the cashier's counter but her arm was too numb to withstand her grasp. She fell against the counter and slid to the ground. The last thing she remembered was being helped onto a stretcher and lifted into an ambulance.

When she awoke, she noticed clean white walls and a leaf-green partition. The rails around her bed were up and she was dressed in hospital attire. She tried to raise herself. She felt heavy, she could barely move. Stuff over which she had no control held her down in bed. She attempted to talk but her lips were numb. She heard chatter. The chatter around her was hushed and unclear.

"David," she tried to say but her speech was not coming out right. She tried to say more words and realized she was slow in forming them. She let her head fall on the pillow. "Where is my husband?" Blossom mumbled.

"How is she, Doctor?" David anxiously inquired of Dr. Hamm.

"Mrs. Clark's blood pressure is not yet under control; hopefully the medicine we've given her will stabilize the pressure."

"I'm sorry Dr. Hamm ... she may have missed a few doses during our recent challenges ... I really should've been making sure she'd been taking her daily dosage." David said.

"She's resting comfortably now, David and that's a good sign, Dr. Hamm said.

"How long will my wife stay here, Dr. Hamm?"

Dr. Hamm looked at David and shook his head from side to side, "We'll keep Mrs. Clark in hospital for a month to observe her recovery ... I must tell you David, your wife may have long term problems ... it may take a year or more for her to make the best possible recovery."

David sighed, "It could've been worse."

TWENTY-EIGHT

Sheldon and Maureen arrived back in Montego Bay from Toronto on a hot and sticky Friday afternoon. It was the first day of a long weekend, and downtown was bustling with shoppers and stragglers. Sheldon had been sitting at the large mahogany desk in his third-floor office thinking about the enormous complications of a Wilbrothers strike.

His phone rang.

"Mr. Doug Williams is calling you, sir."

Sheldon answered. Doug ranted about the tricky situation he had on his hands.

"Doug, my friend ..." Sheldon said, "my worry is that I might have my own labor problems to deal with if my men decide to strike, out of sympathy for your men...You should know, I'm not in the business of hiring so-called scabs. You and I have always been polite when it came to business dealings and I intended to keep it that way."

Doug Williams let out a dry smoker's cough.

"Damn right, Morgan, we don't want to give the guys any reason to stay out longer than necessary."

"I'll instruct my project manager to lock down my West Hill site for the long weekend and hire extra security to maintain order, just in case your men try to get on to my project," Sheldon said.

"Good thinking, Morgan ... Enjoy the long weekend." Doug hung up.

Weariness overtook Sheldon.

"Peggy," Sheldon called out through his slightly open office door, "hold my calls."

Sheldon laid-back in his chair with his head resting on his arms and his legs crossed atop his well-polished desk. He cast his mind back—eleven months? A year? He recalled he had been stewing over his ill-timed decision to marry Blossom's best friend, Maureen Grant. He'd been thinking of ways in which to break the news to Blossom. He was glad when Blossom suggested, by long-distance telephone, that they meet in Montego Bay for a heart-to-heart private conversation. He had hoped in the end he and Blossom would be friends.

Sheldon smiled, when he remembered how right

it had felt when he held her in his arms and made intense love to her. And when they coupled how perfect the aftermath had been.

The intercom on Sheldon's desk rang. "Christ! Peggy, I told you to hold my phone calls."

"Odette Black for you, sir. The call is urgent." Sheldon picked up the phone.

"Hello, Odette."

"Hello, Sheldon; how are you?"

"Very well … How have you and your boys been keeping?"

"We are well, thank you. Sheldon, I'm calling with news that's not so good … I'm sorry to tell you that I just received word from Toronto … Bloss was admitted to Queen's Hospital … She suffered a stroke."

"How could that be? She seemed fine when I saw her in Toronto a few days ago."

"Yes, I know you attended baby Jason's funeral. Bloss suffered a stroke right after the funeral."

"What's the prognosis?"

"I don't as yet have those details, Sheldon."

Sheldon deliberated, "I must go to her."

Sheldon's conscience would not let him turn his back on the woman he couldn't stop loving. The woman who'd carried his child in secret was lying in a hospital bed in Toronto.

"I couldn't live if something bad happened to Bloss," Sheldon said aloud.

He walked over to the large window in his office

and looked down; his SUV was conveniently parked in front of the five-story building. There was a huge sign directly above the building that read "Morgan Construction Company."

He called out to his chauffeur. "Lincoln, I need you to drive me to Sangster's Airport, now."

Sheldon picked up the phone on his desk and phoned home, knowing there would be no one there to answer. He left a message on the answering machine: *Hi Mo, I'm flying to Toronto this afternoon on an urgent matter ... Peggy will fill you in with the details ... bye.* He was lucky to be on a plane in three hours and on his way to Toronto. By the time Maureen picked up the message, he was long gone.

The three-and-a-half-hour flight from Montego Bay to Toronto seemed like forever.

The headache Sheldon had been nursing for the past two days had come back with a vengeance. He adjusted his seat backward.

Upon his arrival in Toronto, Sheldon took a cab from the airport to Queens's Hospital. The cab ride took longer than usual—traffic was heavy along the Queen Elizabeth Way at 6 p.m. He sat in the back seat, fretting about the state in which he might find Blossom. He sighed loudly.

The cab driver looked up into the rearview mirror. He noticed a look of concern in Sheldon's eyes. "Traffic is heavy, sir. We'll get there soon."

"It's not your fault," Sheldon said.

The cab driver was experienced. He knew that

passengers from Pearson Airport didn't usually go directly to a hospital—something terrible must have happened.

A thousand thoughts ran through Sheldon's head as the cab pulled up in front of the hospital entrance. Would Blossom agree to see him? Would he be able to handle seeing her in her condition?

Sheldon paid the fare and gave the driver a tip. He walked into the hospital, a woman at an information desk directed him to elevators and up he went to the sixth floor. He found himself at the front desk of a busy unit with medical staff moving briskly back and forth. He felt lost.

"May I help you, sir?" The receptionist stopped him as he tried to make his way pass her desk.

"My name is Sheldon Morgan; I am visiting Miss Black in Room 603 ... Would you kindly show me to her room?"

"I am sorry Mr. Morgan; Miss Black's husband left specific instructions, no visitors."

"Miss Black would want to see me ... it is very important that I see her; speak with her ... I know she would want to see me," Sheldon went on.

"I'm sorry, sir..." the receptionist said.

A nurse exited room 603.

"I beg your pardon, ma'am, is Miss Black responsive?" Sheldon asked her.

"There are some good signs sir ... she is responding well to medication," The nurse answered.

All of a sudden, David Clark appeared, he had a

scowl on his face. "Morgan, if I find you near my wife or hear that you've visited her while she's here, I will have you arrested for harassment. I hope I've made myself clear."

Sheldon returned David Clark's scowl. "David, my only concern is for Bloss ... this time I will relent, the next time, I'll shove you out of my way and go to her."

Sheldon turned and walked back to the elevators. He kicked at the elevator door as he exited on the ground floor. He was dejected.

Sheldon stood on the curb at the entrance of Queen's Hospital. "Taxi!" he called out.

His journey back to Montego Bay was dreamlike—so much had occurred that would make him re-think his life as he moved forward.

TWENTY-NINE

Blossom was glad to be back in her suite at The Emerald Place after six weeks in hospital. There was much to cope with and the days seemed long.

Each day she contemplated which sorrow she would grieve. Would it be the shocking loss of her son or the damage to her body from the stroke? David was always at her side to comfort her and she was thankful.

"The physiotherapist will be coming in three times a week, honey." David said.

"I will co-operate with the physiotherapist three times a week, David, because it will be good for me," Blossom laughed. Blossom's recovery was occurring quicker than she expected. Within a year, she had regained clear speech and her form was taking its original shape. David was pleasantly surprised by her physical recovery although he knew full recovery might take a longer time.

"Gino ... be a pal, carry on with the delivery of my Friday dinner orders ... My wife isn't well enough to make the trips into your restaurant."

"Very well, Mr. Clark," Gino had replied.

"Honestly, honey," Blossom said, "... I'm learning to cope with the aid of my cane for short trips, and my wheelchair for longer more strenuous movements... we'll be able to go to Gino for our Friday night dinners sooner than you think."

David was pleased with Blossom's progress. "No strenuous movements for my wife ... not yet."

Blossom and David settled down to a life that suited both of them—David wanted to love and care for Blossom and *she* wanted a life of quiet renewal.

Blossom considered how lucky she'd been to have her husband at her side throughout her heartbreaks. In spite of her tragedies, she knew she'd found redemption with David.

On a pleasant Friday evening after David and Blossom had returned home from their dinner at Gino's restaurant, they relaxed with a glass of wine in the solarium of their suite. Afterwards, Blossom felt the need to pleasure her husband. She had not felt that way for many months and she was delighted that her sensations were returning and all was not lost.

David watched his wife as she delicately stretched out in bed beside him, he took her in his arms—contented in knowing he had made her happy. He held her gently against him, kissed her and made love to her in ways he thought he had forgotten. She responded in ways that confirmed her healing.

"Your love is all I need," he whispered in Blossom's ear. Blossom found love on her terms.

Three years passed. Blossom and Lorna Jones had become close friends. "Want to go swimming in the pool downstairs?" Lorna asked Blossom on one of her regular afternoon tea visits.

"What time?" Blossom wanted to know.

"Same time as always." The women laughed.

Lorna, a resourceful woman from Montreal, possibly in her middle thirties when she came to live at The Emerald Place, admitted that her main source of income had been part-time clerical work through temporary employment agencies. Lorna had been sharing her 10th floor suite with her live-in boyfriend Mike Callahan.

Blossom considered Lorna a true confidant, having regard to Lorna's willingness to assist her in every way possible with navigating her wheelchair when she had to be out and about. Blossom studied Lorna, "What does Mike do for a living, Lorna?"

"He's a stockbroker but he's unemployed now."

"Would you and Mike like to come along with me and David to Aruba for a vacation? It will be our treat."

"Thanks a lot, Blossom, I'd love to come with you and David but I'm not sure Mike will agree," Lorna responded.

"Then find out from him ... You and I have been friends for a long time; I do appreciate our friendship, especially the support you've given me during my health challenges ... Please accept this vacation as a gift from David and me."

Blossom and David were happy that Lorna and her boyfriend Mike could be with them in Aruba on their fourth wedding anniversary.

"I would be pleased to hire you as a stockbroker," David told Mike when he submitted an application for the position in David's real estate company. Lorna showed her gratitude by being loyal to Blossom.

Blossom and David spent the following six years devoted to each other. She became a supporter and a major donor to the local paraplegic society and she loved it. He expanded his land development business in Ontario by developing commercial and industrial sites into construction-ready locations.

They spent their leisure time holidaying in their winter home in Collingwood, and their summer home in Ocho Rios but their principal residence was their suite at The Emerald Place. She particularly enjoyed the scenery from the 21st floor.

On a retreat with his project staff in Collingwood, David suddenly became anxious. His new condominium project near Milton posed a challenge from day one. He had hoped the retreat would be a relaxing time of discussions and strategies for a clear way forward but his project manager, Peter Grange, reported challenges that could stymied the project for several months.

Only the day before, David had received word from the property assessment committee at City Hall that was not to his liking.

David telephoned from the cottage retreat. "Honey I'm coming home early … should get home in time for dinner."

"Is everything okay, David?"

"Everything's fine, honey … Peter will wrap things up and bring me up to speed when I see him at the office tomorrow."

David was exhausted. He fell asleep as soon as he came home with a folder containing agreements and purchases lying on his chest. Blossom put the documents in David's attaché case and tucked the covers around him as he slept. She could tell he had been extremely tired.

The following morning, August 25, 2001, David joined Blossom in the solarium; he held a glass of water in one hand and pills in the other.

"Good morning, honey," Blossom said, "here's your cup of tea, your file folder from last night is in your attaché case."

Blossom examined the pills David had in his hand and asked.

"You have a headache, hon?"

"A niggling one since last night ... it usually goes away by noon."

David took two sips from his cup, kissed Blossom and waved goodbye.

After he left, Blossom went down to concierge to receive a package that had been sent to her by express post.

Warm breeze from outside blew into the lobby as residents exited and entered.

"Morning Blossom," Lorna said, her face dripping with sweat from jogging, "I bought you a hot coffee."

"Great ... thank you, Lorna."

The women rode the elevator to their suites.

Blossom prepared her husband's afternoon meal and then examined the contents of the package she'd received, postmarked Venice, Italy, on the front and addressed to Mr. and Mrs. David Clark. It had come from Dana, David's older daughter—a gift of a beautiful antique wall clock. Dana often surprised David and Blossom with gifts from places she'd been vacationing.

Blossom made lunch of tuna on rye, fresh green salad and fruit juice. She and David regularly ate lunch in the solarium and watched traffic.

She looked up at the clock on the opposite wall as it struck half past one. David must be in lunch hour traffic she thought as she rearranged the napkins on the table for the third time. At two o'clock, she phoned David's office.

"Sorry Mrs. Clark, Mr. Clark left for lunch two hours ago." Two-thirty came and David was neither home for lunch nor back at his office. Blossom was concerned.

Around three o'clock, the Concierge buzzed with information that a tenant in Tower 2 reported a car fitting the description of David's car turned crosswise in its underground parking spot. Blossom's heart skipped several beats.

Security and Blossom went to investigate and noticed David's head leaning against the steering wheel. This must be a prank Blossom thought. But it wasn't. The ambulance came. The police came. David had suffered a massive heart attack.

Blossom sat in the lobby of Tower 2 for several hours before she found strength to go up to her suite.

"May I help you?" Lorna Jones asked her softly.

"Yes, thank you Lorna."

The following days were strange for Blossom. She went through what was required of her like a robot.

THIRTY

Friday came with overcast skies and a light drizzle, Blossom planned to be at the funeral home before the mourners so she could be alone with David. She did not look at his body, she wanted to remember him the way he would always be in her heart, vibrant, alive and strong; but more than anything, Blossom was afraid that she would completely lose her mind if she saw David's lifeless body in his casket.

David's funeral mass was held at St. Paul's Anglican Church; he had made that stipulation many years before. The church was full to capacity and flowers were plentiful, everywhere. The service was beautiful. Blossom went up and kissed the casket then she put a single white rose on top of it. Tears were streaming down her face—"I cannot live without him," she whispered to herself.

David's daughters, Dana and Camille were wonderful; they organized a lavish reception for hundreds of mourners. David would have been pleased with the send-off that he received. Blossom moved through the day like a mechanical person, keeping a straight face and being strong.

"I was young too, when I lost my husband," a friend of David's said to Blossom as she mingled at the reception. Blossom smiled, "David was an excellent husband to me."

According to David's wishes, his ashes were poured in the Caribbean Sea.

Dana and her husband Geoff; Camille and her husband Peter; David's best friends Ken Daley and his wife Kathleen; Father Templeton and his wife Sierra, and Lorna and Mike, along with Blossom flew to Montego Bay. They boarded a small yacht that took them out into deep waters. Camille had been carrying the urn that held her father's ashes. Blossom took the urn and handed it to Father Templeton. They joined hands and Father Templeton performed the rite, "Unto Almighty God we commend the soul of David Olson Clark, we commit his ashes to the deep Caribbean Sea." Blossom took the urn from Father Templeton and poured the ashes into the sea.

Local residents who knew David and guests who attended at his burial at sea joined the private reception Blossom's sister Odette organized at their summer home in Ocho Rios. The affair was beautiful.

* * *

Two weeks passed. Blossom's world still felt surreal, she sat in the solarium where she'd ate lunch with David every day since they'd been married. She looked across at Tower 1 and then at Tower 3. She considered David's work in establishing residential, industrial and commercial properties and she marveled at the tremendous legacy he'd left behind.

David Clark's untimely departure under tragic circumstances left a big hole in Blossom's heart. She considered the people whose lives David touched, and she cried mournful tears for her husband. Blossom knew her life would never be the same and she wondered if she could go on living without him. She was missing David, the one person that fate allowed her to call her own. She truly believed fate was making her pay for things she thought she had already recompensed.

It had become challenging to manage without David even with the housekeeper doing chores twice each week. Blossom considered that Lorna Jones would be perfect as her personal assistant. She was delighted when Lorna accepted the offer to assist her on a full time basis. Blossom's trust in Lorna made her the ideal person.

"This offer could not have come at a better time, Blossom," Lorna said.

"I'll make your salary worthwhile, Lorna."

"Thank you very much, Blossom."

"Lorna dear, you've been a real godsend, you comforted me when Jason died, you were with me when I suffered the stroke and, with David gone, who else would I turn to for help? I know ... I would have fallen apart but for the help you've given me." The women smiled together. "You are the right person for me," Blossom went on.

The two women were grateful for what each other offered. The following day was September 11; Blossom had scheduled Lorna to accompany her to her lawyer's office for the reading of David's will.

Blossom recalled bright sunlight streaming into her bedroom through her half open venetian blinds. She opened one eye and then the next and squinted at her alarm clock on the night table. It was 9:15 A.M.

"Darn, the old alarm clock didn't go off again," Blossom said shaking it profusely to generate enough energy to get it going again. Any annoyance that she may have had about oversleeping quickly faded. A good night's sleep was what she needed to ease the persistent pain in her heart over the death of her husband. She felt refreshed.

She reached to answer her ringing phone and accidentally knocked over her unfinished cup of tea from the night before sending liquid splashing on the wall.

"Hello," she said while drying up as much spilled tea as possible.

"Morning, Bloss, this is Lorna are you watching TV?" Her voice sounded urgent.

"No, what's on TV, Lorna?" Blossom asked, easing herself gently to a sitting position on the side of her bed.

"The world is coming to an end, Blossom," Lorna said. Blossom clicked on the TV. She was horrified at what was unfolding. She saw images of planes slamming into the top floors of two very tall buildings in New York and structures crumbling down; the world was perhaps coming to an end.

She opened her blinds fully and looked out into the bright sunshine; and she refused to believe the world was truly ending.

Blossom rested her head in the palms of her hands and thought for a moment. The world was changing and David was not by her side. He would want her to be strong. She remembered his words during her grief over Jason. *"You'll have his memory for a long time, perhaps never go away completely, but you must go on living.*

Blossom's appointment with her lawyer was at 11.30 A.M. Lorna had been waiting in the lobby for her. The drive to Gordon Rusk's Law Office took Blossom and Lorna into rush-hour traffic along Bay Street. Downtown Toronto skies had been clear blue except for thick white vapors spewing out from clusters of high-rise towers. People poured out of Union Station en masse from modes of transportation that brought them into the city from all directions. They'd been rushing madly out into the streets and ignoring *Don't Walk* signs as they ducked into tall buildings that seemed to swallow them up until evening time when they'd be out again to retrace the route that had led them into the buildings.

Where do the huge crowds go once they enter the high-rise buildings? Blossom asked herself. She watched the spectacle from the window of her minivan and sighed. New York was under attack but life goes on elsewhere.

Blossom and Lorna arrived at Gordon Rusk's office on the 10th floor of the Sterling Tower. Lorna settled Blossom comfortably around a large oak table. From her seat by the window, she could see the wide expanse of downtown Toronto.

She noticed a large brown envelope lying prominently in the center of Gordon's desk in front of a gold nameplate that read: Gordon H. Rusk, Q.C. Blossom was glad to have an efficient lawyer like Gordon in charge of David's affairs.

The secretary looked in.

"Please help yourselves to tea and coffee ... fresh donuts are in the box on the side table." Then she pulled her head back into her office and clicked the door shut.

Unexpectedly, David's daughter Dana leaned over, "Hello Blossom, so good to see you again," she kissed Blossom on both cheeks. Camille, David's other daughter mirrored her sister's action. She was hesitant to accept Blossom as a step-mother.

"You both look well." Blossom said. She hadn't seen them since their father's burial at sea. It had been a difficult time for all of them.

Around the table sat David's daughter, Dana and her husband Geoff Wittingham; David's other daughter, Camille and her husband Peter Grange; John and Muriel McNamara, executors of David's Will and, at the back of the room sat a good-looking woman, perhaps in her fifties, and a well-built, older man wearing dark gray pinstripe suit and thick spectacles. Blossom was curious about the couple.

Gordon Rusk was a man in his sixties. He walked into the boardroom wearing gray three-piece suite, looking thinner than how Blossom remembered him at David's funeral Mass. He surveyed the group that sat around the table and cleared his throat several times before he said "Good morning, ladies and gentlemen" in a speech-like manner.

Gordon began his spiel with a quip about David looking down at the faces of everyone in the room and smiling at their reactions when they learned the contents of his Will. Blossom was not amused by Gordon's humor; in fact, Blossom was surprised Gordon was messing around in that manner for David had not been one to make such quips.

Gordon looked closely at each person through his tinted spectacles. There was no need for introductions everyone knew who was who—except for the lady and the gentleman sitting off to the right side at the back of the room.

"Everyone ... Please say hello to Leon Dyce," Gordon said and pointing to the man at the back of the room. "Leon is the lawyer representing Miss Hyacinth Beckford, the lady sitting beside him, in this matter."

Everyone turned their attention to the attractive Hyacinth Beckford outfitted in a lavender skirt suit, powder blue bowl hat with a narrow rim and a thin lavender silk band around the seam of her hat. A small lavender feather was stuck at one side of the silk band.

Hyacinth Beckford raised her head just enough for all to get a glimpse. She held up her right hand and wiggled four fingers in harmony as a kind of "Hi" to acknowledge the attention she was receiving.

Blossom was curious about Miss Beckford and her lawyer.

"Miss Beckford," Gordon Rusk continued, "is the mother of Michael Beckford, David Clark's nineteen-year-old illegitimate son. Michael could not attend the reading of this Will because of a permanent disability that confines him to Tryhall House for disabled persons in Montreal."

A collective "What?!" reverberated throughout the room followed by two or three seconds of silence, then faint whispers and before long audible babble sounded throughout the room.

Lorna looked at Blossom, "Did you hear that?" she said, obviously surprised. Blossom was silent, her eyes firmly glued on Gordon Rusk's tinted spectacles, she was not sure if he'd been looking back at her.

Gordon turned his head in Blossom's direction, possibly acknowledging her stare, and then slowly removed the stack of legal size papers from the large brown envelope.

"Everyone, please ... May I have your attention, please." Gordon was almost whispering.

"This is the Last Will and Testament of me, David Olson Clark ..." Gordon read.

He paused for a moment, raised up from his chair and walked to where Blossom had been seated. He put his hand on Blossom's shoulder, "Are you alright, Mrs. Clark?"

"I am okay, Gordon ... Please proceed with the reading of David's Will," Blossom said.

A secret child was not what Blossom expected to learn about at the reading of David's Will. She looked at David's two daughters; they'd been blowing sniffles in Kleenex. The scene was tense.

Miss Beckford appeared composed with her legs crossed and exchanging whispers with her lawyer Leon Dyce.

"Wonders never cease ...." Lorna whispered to Blossom. "Give it a rest, Lorna ... give it a rest." Blossom whispered back.

"And I give and bequeath, to my darling wife, Blossom, the entire structure known as Tower 2, situated at The Emerald Place in Etobicoke; my winter chalet located in Collinwood, Ontario; my summer home located in Ocho Rios, Jamaica; a fair share of my real estate company known as Greenbelt Real Estate Limited, situated in Toronto; ten percent of Marble & Granite Jamaica Limited situated in Ocho Rios, Jamaica, and unfettered access to the following bank accounts ....

"To my daughter Dana, I give and bequeath...

"To my daughter Camille, I give and bequeath...

"To my son-in-law Geoff, I give and bequeath...

"To my son-in-law Peter, I give and bequeath...

"I leave in trust ... For Michael George Beckford.....

Gordon continued the reading of David's will in total silence. At the end of the reading, everyone stayed stuck on their chair, stunned by the revelation of David's physically handicapped illegitimate son.

It was clear David made sure his estate was divided so that every relative, whoever they were and wherever they may be, had received a decent bequest. Blossom hoped David's gifts would make a difference in the lives of his relatives in his homeland, Jamaica.

In time, Gordon Rusk informed the other beneficiaries of their bequests. Father Templeton was very grateful for the generous gift David bequeathed to his parish.

The consensus had been that Peter Grange be put in charge of the day-to-day operations of David's empire. Peter had good business instincts, as well as basic skills he had learned from watching David. He had already been in charge of operations at Marble & Granite Jamaica Limited in Ocho Rios and doing most, if not all of the travelling that David had done in the past. David would not have objected to Peter running his entire business for he had always thought Peter had a good head. Peter Grange was the right man for the job.

"I will not let the family down ... I'll do my utmost to keep father's legacy intact ... Father's empire will continue to succeed for posterity," Peter Grange assured Blossom.

PART THREE

2002 – 2009

But if you love and must needs have desires, let these be your desires;
To melt and be like a running brook that sings its melody to the night.
To know the pain of too much tenderness.
To be wounded by your own understanding of love;
And to bleed willingly and joyfully.
To wake at dawn with a winged heart and give thanks for another day of loving

—*Kahlil Gibran*, The Prophet

THIRTY-ONE

Spring arrived with persistent fog. The sky stayed dark gray for much of the days. Blossom had been thinking about her mother, and sister. She hadn't seen either of them since David's burial at sea. A vacation at her summer home in Ocho Rios was overdue. She dialed her mother.

"Hello Mom ... I'll be coming home in two weeks, for a break, please tell Cynthia and John to be sure the place is in top notch shape."

"Cynthia does fine housekeeping and John takes good care of the grounds." Margareta Black assured Blossom. She was delighted to know she would be seeing her daughter soon.

"Will you be okay to travel alone?" Margareta inquired anxiously.

"My personal assistant, Lorna Jones goes with me everywhere I go ... she's been a great help to me since David passed."

"Very well, then I'll see you soon."

The day of Blossom's flight to Montego Bay was a wet spring day. The air was damp from the persistent morning rain; mist trickled down her windowpane in long streaks and rays of variegated colors pierced through the thick fog. People carrying umbrellas and wearing colorful raincoats trotted along the sidewalks, unable to escape the sporadic downpours that resulted in splatters from passing vehicles.

On a clear day, if Blossom was sitting in the solarium, she could see sailboats cruising on Lake Ontario—today was different.

The concierge had already picked up their luggage and Blossom and Lorna were ready to take off on their spring break.

Lorna knocked on the door of Blossom's suite and entered. "Good morning Blossom, have you noticed? There is a collision in the intersection."

"I heard the sirens. I didn't bother to look ... there needs to be a stop sign at that intersection." Blossom pulled a light scarf over her shoulders.

Lorna put the kettle on the stove. "Which one ... Earl ... Green ... Chi ...what flavor?" she was holding up the tea bags. "I'll go with Earl this morning ... do we have tea biscuits?" Blossom asked.

"I've got your favorite ... cheese tea biscuits!"

"Very good," Blossom smiled.

The women sat at the kitchen table. "Aren't you delighted that we're going to Ocho Rios, Blossom?" Lorna asked as she sipped.

"I'm thrilled to be leaving this miserable weather behind," Blossom answered with a soft laugh. The intercom in her suite announced the airport limousine had arrived.

Lorna washed and put away the cups. "Let's go Blossom." She assisted Blossom to the elevator and down to the lobby. The limousine had been waiting in the circle at Tower 2.

Blossom and Lorna landed in Montego Bay later that afternoon. When they got to passenger pick up Odette was there to receive them. Odette hugged and kissed Blossom. "So good to see you, Odie ... meet Lorna Jones, my personal assistant."

"Pleased to meet you, Lorna," Odette said.

The women chatted. Lorna made sure Blossom was comfortably seated in the front passenger seat of Odette's late model station wagon.

"This car is very comfy," Blossom observed.

"Had to get one with room enough for my growing family," Odette laughed. The three of them settled down for a leisurely ride to Margareta Black's home.

"Mom planned a reception in your honor tomorrow evening at 6 o'clock, Bloss." Odette said as she pulled into their mother's driveway.

Margareta Black had been standing on the verandah. She was pleased to see how healthy Blossom looked.

"Mom, I'm so happy to see you," Blossom embraced her mother.

"Is everything in fine shape at the house in Ocho Rios?" Blossom inquired excitedly.

"I was in Ochie all week; I made sure the place is ready for you, honey. The helpers manicured the grounds and trimmed the trees ... everything is in ship shape," her mother answered.

Blossom could not talk her mother and sister into cancelling the lavish reception they'd planned for her.

"I prepared a special meal for you Bloss ... escoveitch snapper fish with slivers of red, yellow and green peppers, green onions, shredded carrots and hot seasonings ... the way you like it. And I made you a pumpkin pie using your grandma's recipe." Margareta Black said.

"Thank you Mom, only Grandma Black's pumpkin pie will do for me." Blossom smiled softly when she remembered her grandma's tasty cooking.

The reception was a lovely affair.

It was late when the party was over. Blossom was thankful when friends and well-wishers finally waived their goodbyes and left her alone with her thoughts.

She was remembering other holidays she'd spent in Oho Rios and how lovely they had been.

She quietly withdrew to the inner suite of the cottage, a place where she had found much solace with David, her late husband. Lorna brought her a cup of warm tea. She leaned back in her favorite high back chair, ready to relax for the night.

Margareta Black greeted Sheldon Morgan at the front door, "Come along Sheldon," she said.

"Please accept my apologies for being late, Mrs. Black ... some issues came up that I had to deal with," Sheldon hesitated, "Is Bloss available?"

"She might be a bit tire but I'm certain she won't mind seeing you," Margareta responded.

Sheldon had not seen Blossom since she and David had visited three years earlier.

Margareta and Sheldon entered the inner suite where Blossom sat in conversation with Lorna. She was not aware that Sheldon had entered the room.

Sheldon smiled when he saw Blossom, she was beautiful ... always would be. She was still the one who captured his heart so many years ago. Sheldon stopped short of rushing over to her; he quietly walked into her presence.

"Welcome home, Bloss ... so good to see you," he paused, "... Please forgive me for arriving late."

"Not at all Sheldon ... have a seat, thank you for coming to see me," Blossom smiled.

"I'm truly sorry about David ... When I saw him three years ago he was a picture of good health."

"Sheldon, you're very kind," Blossom smiled. She noticed Sheldon's perfect form, a reminder of her image of him—that was a long time ago, she would not entertain such thoughts.

Lorna Jones stood, "Mrs. Clark ... it is well past your bed time." She moved to the back of Blossom's chair.

"Come back for a visit," Blossom told Sheldon.

"I would like that very much, Bloss," Sheldon said goodnight and left. He was glad to have been in Blossom's company, if only for a short time and happy to have been invited back to see her.

Lorna leaned forward and spoke softly in Blossom's ear, "I heard from a little birdie ... Sheldon and his wife are divorcing."

"Lorna," Blossom paused, "I never understood why you listened to gossip." The women laughed.

"Might not be gossip, Blossom... why else would he visit you tonight if he weren't free."

"It shouldn't matter, Lorna," Blossom smiled.

Blossom and Lorna fell back into their routine when they returned to Toronto. Blossom's charities kept her busy with fundraising events, speaking engagements and social activities.

One morning, shortly after Blossom returned to Toronto from Montego Bay, as she was exiting her suite her phone rang. "Hello"

"Mrs. Clark?"

"Sheldon Morgan? ... What a surprise. Why on earth are you calling me this morning?"

"Because ..." Sheldon let the sentence drop.

"Because what? ... How have you been?"

"Fine ... Working too hard ... I'll be in Toronto in two days. If you are free," he paused, "could we have a bite to eat?"

Blossom heard excitement in his voice. She admitted that Sheldon's presence at her welcome reception in Ocho Rios, though short, lit a spark she thought had died. She had been tempted to say yes when he called two days afterwards to invite her out for lunch. Now he's extending another invitation.

How could lunch or dinner with Sheldon Morgan be a bad thing? Blossom thought.

"Of course I'll have a bite to eat with you, Sheldon. Where?"

"I don't know, you select the restaurant, Bloss."

Blossom laughed. "Okay ... we'll go to Sydney's restaurant for dinner, after we spend some time at the park near to where I live."

"Excellent."

Blossom hoped a reunion with Sheldon would help to erase her painful memories about Jason.

Her eyes fell on Jason's photograph, taken at the age of three-months, set atop the fireplace. Jason would have been about fifteen years old now. She noticed small cracks around the frame. She thought it strange that time had destroyed Jason's picture frame and yet, time left her memories of him untouched. She sighed and headed toward the elevators.

Lorna had been in the lobby, waiting to join Blossom for breakfast at their favorite neighborhood coffee shop. Blossom would've preferred to have breakfast alone but there was no getting away from her regular midweek breakfasts with Lorna.

"Good morning Blossom. I cleared your mailbox. Here's your mail. How's your headache this morning?" Lorna asked.

Blossom made a hand gesture; "It's gone just like that."

Remember, we're going to the spa tomorrow."

"I don't know Lorna... I cleared my schedule for an all-day meeting ... No spa for me," a pleasant smile crossed Blossom's face.

"Blossom, you broke the rule again, you should not be booking meetings without my knowledge, that's the rule. Where will your meeting be and with whom?" Lorna put one foot on the ledge beside the elevator door to lace up one walking shoe.

"I have a meeting with Sheldon," Blossom said.

Lorna turned around sharply, "Sheldon? As in Sheldon Morgan? He wants a meeting with you?"

"Don't be cheeky, Lorna," Blossom tugged sharply on her scarf ... "I have no idea why Sheldon wants to see me ... I'll meet with him ... can't hurt to have lunch or dinner with him."

Lorna laced up her other walking shoe and the two of them went out for coffee. They sat down at their usual table.

"Coffee tastes bitter this morning," Blossom said after she took the first sip.

"Tastes the same as always, Blossom. You say the coffee tastes bitter when something's on your mind."

Blossom looked at Lorna over the rim of her cup.

It was true, since the call from Sheldon about coming to Toronto, she had not been her usual self.

"Let's skip the scones today," Blossom said and moved toward the exit door of the coffee shop.

She and Lorna made their way back to Tower 2. Blossom waved goodbye when Lorna hopped out on the 10th floor, and then continued on to her 21st floor suite. She was truly glad to be getting back so quickly. The rest of the day dragged.

When it was bedtime, Blossom tried to relax with a novel. The novel, and a nightcap, were not doing the trick. Sleep would not come. Blossom could not control her thoughts and so she allowed her thinking to roam; just them the telephone rang.

"Hello".

"Hello Blossom, Lorna here, are you alright?

"I'm fine Lorna, just finishing up a very dramatic chapter in a novel."

Blossom really wanted to be left alone with her thoughts. Lorna sensed Blossom's lack of enthusiasm and said goodnight after a short chat. But Lorna's concern was only for Blossom's wellbeing.

Blossom was almost 54 and she had endured more personal pain than many women at her age.

Blossom tossed and turned without sleep, and then finally she put her housecoat on and went into the kitchen to make another cup of tea.

The light wind that passed through her open window softly caressed her cheeks. A whiff, mixed with exhaust from the nearby petrol station, seeped in with humidity. She closed the window.

At precisely 7.30 A.M., she heard the familiar thud of a newspaper against her door. She picked up her morning paper and turned the pages to the daily horoscope—a daily ritual that would be nonsensical if she did not believe in it.

Her daily horoscope predicted a four-star day. A four-star day prediction was perfect and one that Blossom took seriously.

Buoyed by the fact that Sheldon would be visiting on that day, Blossom entered her walk-in closet and shifted several outfits around to decide which one to wear. She settled on a navy blue silk dress with the matching waist length silk jacket to complete the ensemble.

Lorna had insisted on having tea with Blossom before Sheldon arrived. Blossom had complied. They sat at the table in Blossom's kitchen. The kettle whistled. Lorna laid out two cups and saucers containing earl gray tea bags, and poured out boiling water, the scent of earl gray teased Blossom's senses. She let out a deep sigh.

"Didn't sleep last night?" Lorna asked.

"Not a wink," Blossom admitted.

"You're still in love with Sheldon ... you can't hide it ... you've been wound-up the past two days ... take my advice, Blossom, when you meet with Sheldon, don't let him pull wool over your eyes." Lorna was never shy in giving advice to Blossom.

Blossom thought for a moment then she said, "I'm prepared to consider the part about *wool* over my eyes," the two of them laughed.

"But seriously, Lorna ... I like Sheldon now ... as a friend ... that other part ... the love part ... I'm not thinking about that."

"Be cautious ... I'm not saying he wants your wealth ... he's well-off ... all I'm saying is, listen to what he tells you with caution."

"Lorna dear, I honestly don't know why Sheldon wants to see me, for all I know it's a simple gesture of kindness."

"Fine." Lorna said and made a funny face.

"Lorna ... if I told you once, I've told you a thousand times, I like Sheldon because he's worthy."

"He's worthy? What has he done for you to make him worthy?"

"He is worthy because I am unworthy ... I don't know, ask me another time. This meeting with him has nothing to do with love. And, anyway ... it's not like I am going to marry him." Blossom went on.

"I wouldn't be surprise if you did."

"Lorna, you *kill* me," Blossom sighed. "Why do

you find yourself so deep into my business and who gave you the right to be frank with me?"

Blossom smiled and held up her cup for a refill.

Lorna looked squarely into Blossom's eyes.

"My answer to question one is, I care about you and besides, you let me into your business all the time; my answer to question two is, I'm your best friend, even though I'm your employee, I have every right to be frank with you." They laughed.

"Anyway," Blossom continued, "he is in town on business and we are having lunch, perhaps dinner, who knows?"

The intercom sounded. "Concierge ma'am... Mister Morgan is here."

"Please send him up."

"Yes ma'am."

Lorna swallowed her last sip, "Tell me all about it, and don't leave out detail." Lorna quickly skipped out of Blossom's 21st floor suite and down to her 10th floor suite.

The expected knock indicated Sheldon had arrived. His broad shoulders framed the open door.

"Come in Sheldon," Blossom said.

Sheldon entered. He was holding a long stem yellow rosebud in giftwrap. He had a bright smile and his dark brown eyes twinkled as he came closer. Blossom noticed how his dimpled chin had creased over time. His hair was neatly trimmed, and lightly speckled with gray. His good looks was still striking.

The very light blue shirt he was wearing

underneath his dark blue blazer and his medium gray slacks jolted her memory to the times when every item of clothing he wore made him the object of her admiration. All shades of blue complimented Sheldon's tanned complexion. He was perfect, just perfect. Not showy or over the top flamboyant; just neat and clean cut. And that was what Blossom mostly admired about Sheldon.

With quick steps he walked to where Blossom sat in the solarium.

"Hello Bloss ... so good to see you again."

"Same here Sheldon," Blossom smiled.

Sheldon kissed her lightly on the cheeks.

"Pull up a chair, Sheldon." Blossom pointed to the armchair opposite to where she'd been sitting. Sheldon sat with his legs crossed.

"I was afraid you'd ask me not to come," he said looking intensely in Blossom's eyes. "Would you have told me not to come?" He continued, remembering how tepid she'd been during their brief conversation at her welcome reception in Ocho Rios.

"It would have been ungracious of me to turn down your invitation for a visit; after all, I did extend an open invitation to you when I was in Ocho Rios." Blossom paused. "Mom never told me you would be at my welcome reception; I was surprised to see you, I wasn't sure how to respond. Why did you surprise me like that Sheldon?"

"When my grapevine told me about your reception, my heart would not let me stay away,"

Sheldon answered with a smile. Blossom's eyes could not escape the softness in his dark brown eyes.

"Your grapevine?" Blossom was curious.

"Yes… Your mother would not want me to refer to her as my grapevine… we get along very well … I inquire and she keeps me informed."

Blossom smiled. "So … you're in Toronto on business … yes?"

"Yes, I'm looking to purchase new construction equipment from Caterpillar. I have an appointment with their director of sales at their showroom on Lakeshore Road."

"Good."

"You remember Dixon, my project manager? I brought him along with me … we're staying at the Sutton Place Hotel."

Blossom was delighted to be Sheldon's distraction, if only for a day, having heard his reason for being in Toronto.

Marie Curtis Park was a place where Blossom spent beautiful summer and fall days in the past. She had not been there in a long time and would not mind visiting the park with Sheldon.

Blossom turned in her seat. "Would you like a cup of tea? I love earl gray."

"Yes, thank you. I'll have earl gray as well." Blossom picked up her cane and went to the kitchen.

"Need some help, Bloss?" Sheldon called out.

"No … thank you Sheldon."

She returned with a pot of tea and two cups.

They poured tea and sipped. Sheldon leaned forward. "You have a lovely place, Bloss?"

"I live comfortably here ... more tea?"

"Yes ... thank you."

Sheldon's eyes caught the photograph of Jason on the mantle over the fireplace. He walked to the fireplace, paused for a moment and then touched Jason's photograph. He returned to where he'd been sitting with Blossom. "We're going to the park, yes?"

"Yes." Blossom answered.

Sheldon gently guided her wheelchair into the elevator. The packed elevator made its way down then it abruptly stopped on the 10th floor. *Lorna should already be in the lobby,* Blossom thought, as she peered through the open elevator door to see who was entering.

"Hi Blossom."

Lorna squeezed in behind two other women. She pretended not to notice Sheldon who had been standing at the back.

"Off for a jog?" Blossom asked.

"I'm meeting Winsome in the lobby, we're having a spa day," Lorna said as she rummaged through her purse for an item only she could identify.

"Where are *you* off to?" Lorna asked Blossom; her feeble attempt at being surprise made Blossom smile. Lorna dangled a bunch of keys signifying she'd found what she'd been searching for in her purse.

Blossom was about to reply to Lorna's question when, Sheldon said, "Good morning, Lorna."

Lorna turned around.

"Oh … Good morning Mr. Morgan, nice to see you. When did you come into town?"

"I arrived yesterday, Lorna. Why don't you skip your spa today and come along with Bloss and me… we're off to Marie Curtis Park for a picnic."

"Sorry, Mr. Morgan … no can do."

The elevator reached the ground floor and everyone poured out and scattered.

Across from the public transit station at Long Branch, on the border of Lakeshore Road and Browns Line is Marie Curtis Park, literally a stone's throw from where Blossom lived. When they arrived, Sheldon claimed a wooden table at an ideal spot with a superb view. He opened an umbrella, attached it to a slot on Blossom's wheelchair and neatly arranged the blanket and picnic supplies that Blossom had prepared the night before.

Cool breeze circulated all around the place. Sunlight filtered through leafy branches and the sweet open-air smell of hamburgers and hotdogs was enough to satisfy Blossom's appetite. Nothing had changed at Marie Curtis Park.

"Bloss …over here," Sheldon called out. He had been standing by the fountain watching birds feed on crumbs. There was an air of tranquility about him. The familiarity of his expression brought a gentle quiet sigh to Blossom's chest. He seemed at peace in his world. Blossom wondered how much of their past he'd still hung on to. How much he'd discarded and how much he was willing to talk about.

So much had happened that made Blossom happy yet so much made her want to banish the rest of her life to 'lonely street.'

She did not wish to summon up thoughts about other times with Sheldon; nevertheless, there they were, lodged in her mind, gnawing at her as she watched him move about before her eyes. The truth is they shared a common link. The link was Jason.

She acknowledged a small child touching her arm. "Miss, your shawl was on the ground," the child said and handed the shawl to her.

Sheldon moved swiftly to Blossom's side.

"Are you alright, Bloss," he inclined his head as though to kiss her. She wasn't sure that she wanted him to kiss her although a sudden urge to be in his arms overwhelmed her. Instead, she smiled and assured him all was well.

She remembered the pain of dangerously falling in love with two men at the same time and how she cried tough when she was hurt.

Some of her memories needed a finishing point; a point at which she could be satisfied the hurt had been healed.

Blossom picked up her cane and walked over to her wheelchair. Her wheelchair was evidence of the price she'd paid for loving these two men. It was literally her altar of sacrifice.

Sheldon touched her shoulder. The feel of his touch was strong. Impulsively, she attempted to return the touch; she remembered her promise to Lorna, "*No wool over your eyes.*" Blossom let her hands stay in her lap.

Life should have been kinder, she thought but life gave her what she asked for.

"I am glad you agreed to see me today," Sheldon said as he moved to the back of her wheelchair and eased her gently and deliberately along the soft grass.

"I had a wonderful time," she smiled.

The warm sun beamed from blue summer skies. Blossom acknowledged a greeting from a passing couple with a hand wave.

"I am looking forward to dinner at Sydney's tonight," Sheldon said as he tucked the hem of her long skirt into the side of her wheelchair.

"Me too … I heard that Sydney's is the place to be on a Friday night."

Blossom was pensive. She barely remembered the social graces of being on a date, but Sheldon was different—she had loved him—he had always been the question mark in her life. He had taken her to the peak of their love but she never took off with him and it seemed her life was never complete without him. She drew in a deep breath.

THIRTY-TWO

The summer's evening drive on Yonge Street took Blossom and Sheldon along a corridor of well-lit shops, exclusive boutiques and fancy restaurants with lighted patios. Children strolled with their parents on busy sidewalks, eating ice cream cones. It looked like everyone had come together at Yonge and Dundas Streets.

"There's a celebration going on" Sheldon said.

"It's the Labor Day festivities Blossom observed. She was fascinated by the scenery. At the corner of Yonge and Gloucester was Sydney's, a popular Caribbean restaurant and private club.

Blossom was comfortable wearing a lime green, georgette dress, with a narrow waistband and spaghetti shoulder straps. Her diamond-studded cross necklace matched the diamond stud earrings in her ears. Her hair hung loosely just above her shoulders. Her toes peeped out through black satin slippers.

Sheldon turned an admiring side-glance at Blossom and smiled. He was pleased to have her seated beside him.

When they arrived, Sydney's Restaurant was already buzzing with patrons. Sheldon guided Blossom's wheelchair gently along the aisle and between tables and chairs.

Seated at a table to the left of the entrance, were Father Templeton and his wife Sierra.

Father Templeton had become a close friend of Blossom and he considered it his duty to *guide* her after the death of her husband David, having regard to David's generous bequest to the church.

The waiter made his appearance with the dinner menu and wine list after he'd seated Blossom and Sheldon comfortably in the private booth reserved for them. They ordered the beef pot-roast, with a medley of steamed vegetables and a side order of baked sweet potatoes.

Sheldon was pleased that the bottle of chilled champagne that he'd painstakingly selected arrived first. With a light pop, Sheldon uncorked the champagne bottle sending squirts of bubbly all over the dining table.

"To your health," Sheldon said.

"And to yours," Blossom responded.

The evening was delightful, with music from the 80's and 90s. The noise level had increased several notches as music blended with laughter and chatter. The song: *Warm and Tender Love,* by singer Percy Sledge was playing and couples were dancing.

Sheldon dabbed the corner of his mouth with his napkin, pushed back his chair and escorted Blossom to the dance floor. He kept a firm hand on her waist, holding her to him for balance. They slow-danced to a set of songs that brought back wonderful memories for both of them.

"You were graceful on the dance floor." Sheldon whispered to Blossom after he escorted her back to her seat at the table.

He poured himself another glass of champagne.

"May I pour you some more champagne?" he asked Blossom and she answered yes.

Blossom's eyes caught Father Templeton as he strolled over to her table "I've been watching you *kids*…you're having a jolly good time!" he said.

"Father Templeton … please meet Sheldon Morgan, a dear friend," Blossom said.

Father Templeton chuckled and held out his hand, "Your dear friend is my dear friend Mrs. Clark …I'm pleased to meet you Mr. Morgan." He smiled and left them alone.

Sheldon turned to face Blossom, his voice was low. "There is something I've been wanting to tell you Bloss." She leaned-in to hear him clearer.

"My divorce is final." Sheldon sounded happy.

Blossom remained still.

"My desire is to have you … to make you a

permanent part of my life. I love you Bloss … always will … why you? Because you're a good woman and I believe you were meant for me," he broke off. He remembered the many times he had asked Blossom to marry him and all of those times she'd asked him to wait.

"There is no need for us to wait … we love each other … this is the way it ought to be. Let's be together as husband and wife … I will only accept a resolute yes"

Sheldon paused, realizing he had been talking without a response from Blossom. He bit his lower lip and then he went on.

"But if you tell me you don't want me I'll leave and never try to see you again." Sheldon's determination moved Blossom.

Yes, she had loved him at the height of her desire, she had had his child to complete her love for him and, up to this point, she had re-lived every wonderful moment they had spent together.

There were roadblocks and disappointments. Some things happened that made them angry with each other; other things happened that made Blossom angrier with herself. They'd burnt their challenging bridges and swallowed their bitter pills.

Lorna Jones had earlier warned Blossom about accepting Sheldon back into her life. Lorna exhorted her to consider carefully any pitch that Sheldon may put forward to sway her thinking. Blossom admitted she'd loved Sheldon in the beginning as she loved him in the moment. There was no need for Sheldon to make a pitch or pull *wool* over her eyes; she belonged to him. Why else had he come back after such adverse circumstances?

Blossom realized she had pushed Sheldon around far too long. The tone in his voice alerted her, this was no longer a game of *more time*. This might be her last chance to have the man she truly loved. She was ready to say yes to Sheldon—his wife is what she'd always wanted to be.

"Yes, my love … I'll marry you … if you'll have me the way I am."

"Dearest … you've made me the happiest man, I love you, Bloss…The question is; will *you* have me now?"

"I never stopped loving you, Sheldon … I zigged and zagged all this time and now I have you."

Sydney's was almost empty. The bartender was wiping down the counter. Sheldon took Blossom's hands in his, he remembered the times he had had her and the completeness he enjoyed.

"I've tasted your love … I have enjoyed the flavors … it's bitter and it's sweet, there are no secrets between us," he paused. "I am a lucky man for I now have everything I ever wanted."

Blossom remained silent.

"I'll take you home my love," Sheldon said and navigated Blossom gently to his rental car. He kissed her goodnight in the lobby and requested the night guard to guide her to her suite.

Blossom tossed and turned in bed; sleep would not come. She had made several cups of tea already, another cup of chamomile tea won't hurt. The tea didn't diminish her desire for Sheldon. It had been many years since Sheldon made love to her but the memories were fresh and real. She was nervous, she was not sure she could be the wife he expected her to be. She sighed.

Sheldon laid-back on the chaise in his suite at the Sutton Place; the thought that soon Blossom would be completely his sent him to the showers to subside his desire.

He tossed and turned; sleep would not come.

At last, morning came.

The phone in Blossom's suite rang. She answered.

"Good morning, my love ... did you sleep well last night?" Sheldon asked.

"I didn't sleep a wink, I was up all night thinking about you," Blossom admitted.

"Me too," Sheldon groaned lovingly.

"Let's have breakfast at Sydney's," Blossom said.

"Sounds delicious ... I'll come and get you."

They had breakfast cereal of corn meal, light toast, boiled eggs and a variety of fruits.

After they'd eaten, Sheldon pulled a small box from his side pocket and exposed a ring with an enormous diamond.

Blossom gasped.

"I've been wanting to put this ring on your finger for a long time and every time I tried, things got in the way ... there are no obstacles in the way now," he slid the ring on her finger.

"Sheldon, this ring is gorgeous ... I love you so much."

THIRTY-THREE

"Dixon ... relax," Sheldon told his project manager, "the machinery and equipment we purchased from Caterpillar won't get down there before 90 days anyway ... carry on until I come ... I will be back in time to receive the equipment off the docks."

The men talked about more business matters before they hung up.

Sheldon took up temporary residency at the Sutton Place Hotel to be with Blossom. They re-acquainted themselves and spent the following eight weeks in total bliss.

They enjoyed intimate dinners, quiet teas; entertaining theatre visits, long outings, and lazy afternoons just being in each other's company. Their time together was therapy for both of them.

Blossom and Sheldon had been sitting on the balcony of Sheldon's suite at the Sutton Place Hotel. He was doing a word puzzle and she was reading a novel. He raised his head and looked at her.

"Honey ... who said these words, *"Love has no other desire than to fulfill itself."*

She smiled and answered, "I believe it was Gibran, *Kahlil Gibran.*"

"You're correct." They laughed.

Sheldon leaned over and bruised Blossom's lips with a kiss, she felt a bit shy; it had been a long time since she'd been kissed like that. She panicked. She might be experiencing cold feet or having second thoughts. She acknowledged that both of them carried wounds from their previous relationships. Still, she felt safe; she relaxed when she remembered how happy she had been the other times when she was with Sheldon. It seems like she was falling in love with him all over again.

Sheldon picked up her vibes. He was unsure of an approach. He knew that pieces of their lives had been lying dormant for many years; he decided those pieces were worth picking up. He shifted.

"Honey, let's make love" he whispered.

"Sheldon I don't know…" Blossom let the rest of the sentence fall off.

"I understand, my love. I'm tense too; we'll work things out together, starting now."

"I don't remember how to please you Sheldon."

"It'll come back sweetheart." Sheldon lifted her

tenderly and carried her into his suite. He kicked the door shut. The tiny buttons on Blossom's shirt were *calling* him to release them; he set them free, one by one. Her creamy breasts lay bare before his eyes. He felt a strong desire to have them. When he lifted his head from her ever beautiful breasts they were both overwhelmed with desires that were pushing them to a place they once knew.

He pleasured her to her heart's content. When he was certain that her needs were completely met he took her with all of the strength he could muster and enjoyed every moment of the beautiful body she presented to him.

"I love you Sheldon," she moaned to his delight as they collapsed in each other arms.

"I will miss you very much when I leave tomorrow. I never thought I could enjoy more happiness with you than I already enjoyed," Sheldon paused, "Bloss ... come to me soon."

Sheldon returned to Montego Bay. Blossom followed shortly thereafter with a visit to her summer home in Ocho Rios.

"I'll create a new setting—one that's in keeping with my new outlook on life," Blossom told Sheldon when she arrived in Ocho Rios. She requested an interior decorator to re-decorate the inside of the cottage and additional people to maintain and upkeep the property. Fresh, firmly matted green grass covered the yard to accommodate Blossom's easy access. Well-kept rose bushes were all around the grounds. Shrubs and shade trees made the yard cool and comfortable. Everything was as Blossom desired.

Lorna agreed to stay in Ocho Rios for an extra month to assist in re-organizing and redecorating the place. Blossom decided she would spend much of her time in Ocho Rios.

When it was time for Lorna to return to The Emerald Place, Blossom gave her additional duties. Some of her new duties were to make sure that Suite 2108 and her winter home in Collingwood were kept clean and well-maintained at all times.

Blossom requested Lorna to order new rugs from a Persian rug store in Toronto, and ship them to her in Ocho Rios as soon as possible.

"It will be different for me when I move about The Emerald Place. I'll miss you, Blossom."

Blossom smiled, "You are who I depend on to simplify my busy schedule ... just think how different it will be for *me* without your help." The women hugged before they said goodbye.

Odette assumed Lorna's role as Blossom's personal assistant while Blossom stayed in Ocho Rios. The sisters were happy to be together again. "Bring Mom along with you next time, Odie ... I'll need both of you here to help me plan my wedding."

Blossom kept busy with the planning of her wedding. She requested the ballroom at Moonbeams-

On-The-Hill to be converted into a beautiful chapel, decorated with roses.

The entrance into the chapel was an arch of rosebuds and blooms of many colors. The pews were tied with big bows of pastel colors entwined with rosebuds.

Margareta Black laid Blossom's wedding dress across the bed. The outfit was a light beige calf-length brocade dress, designed with cap sleeves and high neckline with tiny pearl buttons down the back.

On the day of her wedding, she wore a matching pair of slippers decorated with pearl droplets. Her headdress was a Tiera covered with pearl beads and champagne color rosebuds. She placed a bouquet of multicolored roses, decorated with streams of silk ribbons, in her lap.

"Something old and something borrowed will be my surprises for you, Bloss," Margareta said and kissed her daughter lovingly.

Margareta was delighted to witness Blossom's nuptials.

On June 3, 2004, on the 54th birthday of Blossom Mae Black, she and Sheldon Jason Morgan were joined together in holy matrimony. It was a beautiful sunny day. Blossom wore her hair on her shoulders. She was a beautiful bride.

Sheldon stood at Blossom's side in formal attire, with a yellow rose sprig on his lapel.

Sheldon's mother performed the wedding ceremony. The vows they said were unstructured.

There were cries, sighs, smiles and outright laughter. It was a significant occasion in the life of Blossom and Sheldon.

Guests included Margareta Black; Odette and her husband Winston and their children; Boyd Stephenson and his wife Delores and their children; Lorna Jones and Mike Callahan, and many others. It was a day of love, dreams fulfilled, family, and merriment.

Mother Morgan gave a lighthearted lecture about the do's and don'ts of married life to the delight of everyone. Blossom had found love at last, in the arms of Sheldon Morgan.

During the following six years she lived in her summer home in Ocho Rios and her retreat home in Collingwood, Ontario. But she mostly enjoyed her condominium suite at The Emerald Place in Etobicoke, Ontario.

Blossom devoted much of her time and money to charities for the disabled. The residents of Ocho Rios and surrounding areas benefitted from her work in transforming public buildings into accessible places for disabled customers. With Sheldon by her side, Blossom was happier than she'd ever been.

One afternoon as they relaxed in the flower garden at the Ocho Rios home, Sheldon was matter-of-fact.

"I should spend more time with you, honey," he said. Blossom laughed. "You've spent a lot of time with me, dear, and anyway, I've been busy with my philanthropic work."

"That is true, and you love your work very much."

Sheldon was proud of Blossom's outspokenness on accessibility. He watched her as she leafed through her datebook and organizes her schedule

"Honey, we leave for Toronto next week Thursday, for a month," Blossom said.

"Great ... thanks for the reminder ... I love fall in Toronto ... when the leaves begin to change colors and the temperature gets cooler ... We'll stay for more than a month so we have extra time with friends." Sheldon went on.

"Come, my dear ... Lets have dinner on the patio ... Mom made your favorite casserole, with lots of spices."

"I'm starving, I can't wait to eat."

Over dinner, Blossom and Sheldon discussed their trip to Toronto.

"And while we're in Toronto I'll book an appointment for my annual check-up with Dr. Steiner although it will be a month early."

"Excellent idea."

When they reached Toronto, Blossom promptly called for an appointment with Dr. Steiner, her family doctor.

"Dr. Steiner will see you tomorrow at noon, Mrs. Morgan," said the receptionist.

At Blossom's check-up, Dr. Steiner ordered several tests.

"We'll still be in town when the results come back, Dr. Steiner," Blossom said with a laugh.

Sheldon had just come in from his morning walk. "I brought your coffee, honey."

"Thank you, Sheldon … Dr. Steiner's office called while you were out … he wants us to come to his office tomorrow at 9 o'clock in the morning for the results of my tests."

"Then we'll be at his office tomorrow morning at 9 on the dot," said Sheldon and kissed Blossom on the cheeks.

"I hope the tests are fine," Blossom said.

"It'll be fine, honey," Sheldon put an arm around Blossom's shoulders.

Dr. Steiner greeted Blossom and Sheldon with a smile; he kept up a light conversation about the weather and compared the cool fall in Toronto to the warm all-year-round weather in Montego Bay.

"I'll take the weather in Montego Bay every day of the year," Dr. Steiner said.

He opened a folder in front of him.

"Now … let's talk about your results." Dr. Steiner turned several pages.

"We discovered the onset of an illness that attacks soft tissues," Dr. Steiner was looking directly at Sheldon as he spoke, "… this is a progressive disease, Blossom will likely lose more muscle mass and strength." Dr. Steiner paused for Blossom and Sheldon to grasp what he'd said. He continued, "There's good news, though … there is breakthrough medicine to slow down its progress." Blossom stared blankly at Dr. Steiner. Sheldon appeared shocked.

"We'll stay here for treatment," Sheldon said to Blossom without inquiring from Dr. Steiner how long her treatment would take.

Weeks later, Sheldon had been out on errands, and Lorna Jones had come up to Blossom's suite to go over clerical matters. The women had been sitting in the solarium. Suddenly Lorna noticed Blossom slouched in her wheelchair. At first Lorna thought Blossom had dozed off but she soon realized something was wrong.

Unexpectedly, Sheldon walked into the suite. He rushed to Blossom's side and immediately called an ambulance. Blossom was taken to Queens Hospital— she had suffered a second stroke.

Sheldon was constantly by her side when she was in Queens Hospital. One day he looked at her and said. "We're in this together, honey."

"Our life has taken another turn," Blossom said in response.

"Not a destructive stroke," Dr. Steiner told Sheldon when they met to evaluate Blossom's condition, "... however, the disease we discovered will likely slow down her recovery from her stroke."

Sheldon decided not to return to Montego Bay without Blossom. He communicated everyday with Michael Dixon, his project manager.

"I'm confident you and the rest of staff will manage okay... I'm only a phone call away, Dixon."

THIRTY-FOUR

Sheldon wished Blossom hadn't put on the hospital attire she had worn out of discharge. She seemed to have grown comfortable wearing those hospital gowns even though she didn't like them at first.

Blossom would not readily admit to it but she hated the white walls, the railings around her bed and the green bedding she had had to endure for several weeks when she was in the hospital. She was happy to be home again.

"Let's dress you in one of your frilly statin gowns today, honey" Sheldon said after he had bathed and perfumed her.

"I like the other ones better, Sheldon ... there are no clasps or buttons to contend with," she laughed.

For the most part, Blossom had not been able to

move about without the use of her wheelchair and the latest stroke, coupled with her weakening muscles, left her incapable of doing many things for herself.

She pondered her illness. Her condition was evolving beyond her control although Dr. Steiner had been trying the new breakthrough medicine which he believed would slow down her deteriorating muscles.

"We'll see this through ... together ... you and I," Sheldon said to Blossom in a quiet moment when they sat in the solarium.

"I don't know, Sheldon, this time it's more overwhelming. I probably will not survive the shock. It is really becoming too much for me to endure."

"We'll survive." Sheldon pressed Blossom's head to his chest and kissed the top.

"I've been feeling far more tired of late ... I will rest a while in the solarium," Blossom said. Sheldon lifted her gently and arranged her in the love seat.

Blossom's team of doctors met and decided that her personal care was foremost. Dr. Lee-Ho, Blossom's psychologist called to give her the good news—she had located a well-run convalescent home in a quiet neighborhood in Etobicoke that provided top-notch care.

"Ethica Mature Lifestyles is the Rolls Royce of homes," Dr. Lee-Ho told Blossom. "The staff is excellent. I am certain you will be happy during your convalescence at Ethica."

Blossom and Sheldon visited the facility and fell in love with it. The place was beautifully decorated with paintings and pictures on the walls. The color scheme in her quarters was light gray and pastel green. Fine carpeting and colorful rugs adorned the floor. Everything was of fine quality. There was a mock fireplace in Blossom's personal sitting area.

"That was my special request for you, Bloss." Sheldon kissed Blossom.

"Jason's photograph will look superb over the fireplace," Blossom said.

"Most definitely," Sheldon replied.

They both decided Ethica was a good place for her recovery. Physical therapists and additional personal support workers were available to assist Blossom in her rehabilitation. She was hopeful, that before long she would return to the warmer climes of Ocho Rios to live the rest of her life with her husband.

The day came.

Blossom woke up feeling like she'd been sleeping too long although she knew she'd been up all night.

All of this is a terrible dream ... I'll wake up soon. Why are the people in my dream so real and alive and my body so old and wrinkled?

The *why* questions troubled her. Blossom closed her eyes then she opened them again. She looked at her reflection in the mirror on her bedside table—she'd intentionally turned over every mirror in her suite so she wouldn't see her reflection. Now she was ready to examine her arms, her legs, and her entire body—her beautiful body had deteriorated right before her eyes, she'd watched it happen like a helpless bystander.

The thud against Blossom's front door jolted her to new realities that confronted her. Lucy, the papergirl, had brought the morning paper. Blossom wanted to read the day's horoscope. She wanted the forecast to be a five star day.

She turned to see if Sheldon had been lying in the twin bed next to her. The bed was empty. Sheldon was probably at the nearby bakery picking up freshly baked pastries; likely, the last time he would be required to do such a chore.

She looked around her suite; a thin layer of dust was on the ledge of her window. It had become more and more difficult for Sheldon to keep up with house duties in-between Lorna's visits.

The last of the nightshade disappeared. From her favorite spot at the bay window in her solarium, Blossom gazed out to the silent gray lake. There were no sailboats, at least not yet. With the rising of the sun, the lake would be dotted with sailboats, a sight forever fixed in her memory. She looked down at the freeway, as always, it was full of activity.

The idea that her world had evolved to a place where she was no longer in charge was frightening.

Blossom fancied a cup of tea with her confidant,

Lorna Jones, but Lorna had moved to her new home in the town of Milton, too far for a quick cup of tea.

"Your grandson turned 23 last month, Mom," Dana had said to Blossom during tea when she had come to visit. Blossom was ecstatic that Dana had recognized her as *Mom*.

"How is it possible that Christopher reached 23, where was I when he was growing up?" Blossom enquired of Dana—tongue-in-cheek.

"You were enjoying life, Mom." The women laughed. Blossom knew her late husband David Clark would have been proud to know Dana called her *Mom*. David's other daughter Camille, never got to the place where she called Blossom *Mom*. Sweet Camille, no woman could take the place of her mother. Camille had her own two daughters and Peter Grange, her husband, was still in charge of David's empire.

Blossom looked back, with less regret than most people who knew her would have expected or even imagined. She was 60, life had given her plenty yet life had taken back much. Blossom was ready to embrace the newness of her present condition. Her stay at the convalescent home would be different from what she had known and grown used to. "And you'll stay here only until you've regained your strength honey ... then I take you home," Sheldon assured Blossom.

Sheldon at 64, presented well; his neatly cut hair—the thing Blossom loved most about him—turned salt-and-pepper in color. His shoulders still straight and strong. He had all of the features that first attracted Blossom to him.

Blossom surveyed the inside of suite 2108. She touched the greenery, every leaf, every flower; she ran her fingers along the frames of her paintings and lingered at the ones by her favorite painter—Escoffrey. She stayed a moment at elaborate pieces of furniture; she sank her toes in Persian rugs, and she traced her fingers across the mantle of the fireplace. Then, she removed the photograph of Jason, at three months old from the mantle. He would have been about twenty-two years old now, doing the things that young men at his age do. His shoulders would have been square just like Sheldon's; his chin might have been dimpled.

The imagery would forever be a fantasy.

She folded several sheets of tissue paper over Jason's photograph and put more sheets of paper beneath to protect it during travel.

Breakfast was oatmeal cereal, two hard-boiled eggs, buttered croissants, black coffee and orange juice. She sat at the kitchen table and waited for Sheldon to return from the bakery.

Several pieces of luggage that Sheldon packed the night before was stacked at the door of her suite, to be collected by the door attendant.

Blossom picked up the phone on the kitchen wall

and dialed her sister. Odette answered.

"Hello Bloss, good to hear you, when I phoned yesterday Sheldon said you're recovering well."

"That's true ... *I am* feeling a lot better ... John phoned me from New York to tell me he and Nancy are expecting a baby ... I'm so happy for them ... my grand-nieces and grand-nephews are adding up."

"That's right. With Frankie's two girls; Matthew's three boys and a girl ... soon you'll have seven grand-nieces and grand-nephews combined."

The sisters laughed.

"It is so good that Mom got to know her great-grandchildren."

"She enjoys them when they visit although her eyesight is not as sharp ... Your hip joints ... are they still stiff, Bloss?"

"I've learned to live with the stiffness ... You and Mom should stay at the summer home in Ocho Rios as often as you like ... I go to the convalescent home starting today and I would like both of you to keep the lights on and the rooms warm for me until I return." Blossom laughed.

"I love you, Bloss," Odette's tears streamed down her cheeks and landed on the phone in her hand as Blossom spoke. The sisters had carried their love and friendship through the twists and turns of their lives. The reality of Blossom being in an unfamiliar place was overwhelming for Odette. Her hand shook as Blossom went on.

"Sheldon will be travelling between Montego Bay

and Toronto during my period of recovery—it will not be an easy task for him ... tell Mom to take care of him for me."

"Mom and I will look after him, Bloss." The sisters laughed.

"Be sure to leave me a phone number ... so we can have our regular chats." Odette said to Blossom.

"I couldn't survive without our chats, Odie."

"Ta-ta, Bloss."

"Ta-ta, Odie. Kiss Mom."

That Sunday afternoon in early November was sunny and the temperature was right. The sky was bold azure with fluffy white clouds drifting in the atmosphere. Blossom imagined being on a picnic with her husband, Sheldon at Marie Curtis Park. But her day dream came to an abrupt end when a small bus with the words: *Ethica Mature Lifestyles* inscribed on both sides appeared in The Emerald Place roundabout. It stopped in front of Tower 2 lobby. Sheldon recognized the small bus.

"Shall we go, honey?" he said softly.

Blossom looked up into his eyes. Sheldon slowly knelt by the side of her wheelchair. He pressed her hands against his heart.

"We'll be together soon," he said.

Blossom sighed.

The lift raised her wheelchair gently into the bus.

The attendant settled her comfortably. Sheldon stood on the curb—waving.

"I love you," Sheldon mimed.

"I love you too," Blossom mimed back.

The small bus moved out gently on to the freeway en route to a new place and perhaps a new beginning.

Like sheaves of corn he gathers you unto himself.
He threshes you to make you naked.
He sifts you to free you from your husks.
He grinds you to whiteness.
He kneads you until you are pliant,
And then he assigns you to his sacred fire,
That you may become bread for God's sacred feast.
All these things shall love do unto you that you may know
the secrets of your heart.

—*Kahlil Gibran,* The Prophet

EPILOGUE
Ethica Mature Lifestyles, 2011

She touched her hair and straightened her drooped shoulders. It seemed like she'd been waiting a long time for Sheldon to come for her. Blossom had promised him she'd wait until the *12th of Never*, and that's a very long wait.

She pressed the phone to her ear.

"Hello Odie, how are you?"

"So-so, Bloss, I am calling to tell you…."

The evening sun receded, night-lights started to come on. Blossom had been in the rose garden for several hours. "It is time for your evening meal, Mrs. Morgan," her attendant whispered softly before she navigated Blossom to the dining room.

She pulled a wrinkled page from her purse. The blue lettering on light gray, tear-stained paper was fading. She sighed. She'd already memorized every word:

Montego Bay,
June 3, 2009

My darling Bloss,
I am counting the days until I see you. It won't be long before I return for you; I will have you in my arms, where you belong. I love you so much.
Your husband,
Sheldon

ACKNOWLEDGMENTS

Thanks to Blossom Mae Black, a fictional character nonetheless, who'd been with me as I defined her in *Cry Tough*; to my readers for patiently waiting to read *Cry Tough*; to Christina Dudley, for her timely critiques of *Cry Tough*; to Cheryl Antao-Xavier for editing *Cry Tough*; to my daughter, Sharon Laing for cheering me on; and to my husband for giving me the latitude to put pen to paper.

Olive Rose Steele

ABOUT THE AUTHOR

Olive Rose Steele is mother of one and grandmother of two. She spends most of her time writing Fiction and Non-fiction books.

Olive's first published work; *And When We Pray* (Suggestions and prayers for living in spirit) is her flagship Non-fiction book. *Great is thy Faithfulness* (Insights for seekers of self) is her second Non-fiction book.

Cry Tough is a romantic, suspense Fiction Novel.

She received Honorable Mention in the 2014 Mississauga MARTY Award in the Emerging Literary Arts category for her literary work.

Olive resides with her husband in Ontario, Canada.

WATT TOWN ROAD
(A Memoir*)*

OLIVE ROSE STEELE

Coming Spring, 2015

CHAPTER 1

Me alone / Pon Watt Town Road / although the road may be rocky and steep / With mi bible in mi hand / and mi wrap around mi head / Me alone pon Watt Town Road
—Sung by Eugenie Beatrice Brown

I was six years old. As I recalled, everyone in the community of Sandy Gully was sad, something terrible had happened. The grown-ups ignored me when I asked why everyone was so sad—what had happened was a grown-up matter, I was told. Later, my aunt Mamas said old man Lester fell off the footbridge to his cabin, into Wobble creek and he was swept into the raging Wagg River. The whole neighborhood was in grief.

Lester King lived in Sandy Gulley for as long as everyone living in the village remembered. He knew everyone—young and old, and everyone knew him.

Mister Lester, as I called him, was a loyal friend of my grandparents; he was a regular visitor to our yard and a lead worker on my grandparent's farm.

He was like family.

The name I remembered people called Mister Lester, was *One finger Lester*. It baffled my immature infant brains that he answered to that name for I counted eight fingers and one thumb on his hands.

It had rained for a week, gullies, creeks and streams were overflowing, and rushing madly downstream.

The entire village battened down in Teacher Bailey's schoolroom, at the top of the hill.

Miss Rozlynn, my grandmother's best friend called out for grandmother, to join the village residents in the schoolroom for safety.

"Genie, Mr. Malcom's shop is under water and teacher Bailey say we go up to school fa safety."

"Don't need to Rozlynn ... mi live pon hill and de house top, no leak."

My grandmother was more concerned about the safety of Lester King whom she knew had been out of the village on business and would have had to cross the footbridge to get to his cabin. "Lester come back yet? grandmother inquired of Miss Rozlynn.

"Don't see im" Miss Rozlynn answered and quickly totted off.

Grandfather made it home safely that day. He stepped onto the verandah with a sack on his back. He threw down the sack of sweet yams and potatoes in one corner on the verandah. Grandfather rested his hat on the table and wiped dripping rainwater from his forehead. When he pulled his rubber boots from his wet feet I ran to grandfather with his slippers.

"Genie," he said, "Roslyn's grandson, Calvin say he si Lester crossing di footbridge, he see im fall down in Wobble creek and wash 'way."

"Say wat Gladstone?" grandmother came running out to the verandah, the rain was coming down heavily and thunder was rattling.

"A don't believe im Genie … di likkle bwoy tell stories … anyway, Lester is good swimmer. Three days later, after the rain had stopped, Mister Lester's body was discovered, washed up on the banks of the Wagg River, three miles downstream.

In recognition of his loyalty my grandparents, donated a burial spot on their farm for Mister Lester's interment. Grandmother was still crying many days after his death.

My aunt Mamas told me that when Mister Lester drowned in Wobble creek he was 66 years old and still the most suitable bachelor in Sandy Gully. She said Mister Lester looked very good for his age, he carried himself well, and he lived alone in his cabin on the other side of the creek. It was no secret, Mister Lester didn't have to remain a bachelor for up until his untimely demise, he turned the heads of the ladies in Sandy Gulley. And, apparently, in his younger years, Mister Lester desired a certain lady who lived in Sandy Gully, whom he could not have, and he vowed he would never consider any other woman. Mister Lester remained single and lived by himself until that fateful rainy day when he attempted to cross over the raging Wobble creek on the narrow footbridge to his cabin; a journey he had taken several times before, in all kinds of weather. Poor Lester King, he returned to his Maker without the love of his life—or perhaps not.

NON-FICTION BOOKS BY OLIVE ROSE STEELE

And When We Pray:
Suggestions and Prayers for Living in Spirit

First published work by Olive Rose Steele, *And When We Pray* is a book of prayers and suggestions on how to deal with the challenges of day-to-day living. *And When We Pray* includes many logged prayers from Steele's prayer journal. She reveals, with honesty, her faith in prayer and encourages readers to rely on the awesome power of their prayers.

Great is Thy Faithfulness:
Insights for Seekers of Self

Once again, Olive Rose Steele demonstrates her unique style of expressing the issues of life and showing how her challenges mirror the challenges of others in much the same manner. *Great is thy Faithfulness* expands on her thoughts on the awesome power of prayer. First recognized in her flagship publication *And When We Pray,* in *Great is Thy Faithfulness* Steele explains how true Self may tame Ego's desire to divide and conquer. Steele encourages readers to make prayer the centerpiece of daily life.

Made in the USA
Charleston, SC
03 February 2015